Blog Post Mortem

Mark Berkeland

Blog Post Mortem

Mark Berkeland

Chapter 1

Blog Entry Number One:

Today I went to the store. Okay, perhaps this isn't the most auspicious way to start an exciting new venture, such as this blog...I mean, we *all* go to the store, right? Why would anyone want to read about something we *all* do, something common and ordinary and mundane? The phrase "I went to the store" just drips "boring" from every literary orifice. And, to compound matters, why would anyone want to read about "dripping orifices?" Are you still here? Why?

Perhaps I should start again, give it a bit more "zing" (and a bit less "drip")...

It was a desperate situation...hunger was setting in like a bad case of gangrene, and my stockpile of consumable goods was shrinking alarmingly low. "Not good," I muttered, between the blaring gurglings of my emaciated bowels, "not good at all." My options were limited; die a slow, agonizing death of malnutrition, or somehow overcome my overwhelming peckishness and venture forth into the world, seeking solace and comfort in an establishment specializing in comestibles.

Whoa. That really sucked. Perhaps "Today I went to the store" wasn't so bad after all.

Today I went to the store. Not just *any* store, mind you, but the *grocery* store. And not just *any* grocery store, mind you, but the B&G Supermart. And not just *any* B&G Supermart, mind you, but the B&G Supermart near my house. And not just *any* B&G Supermart near my house, mind you, but...well, technically, there is on-ly one B&G Supermart near my home, the one at Sixth and Jackson, so I suppose it *would* be *'any'* B&G Su-permart near my house (mind you). But I digress. Get used to it.

They like me there at the ol' B&G Supermart. Perhaps it is my quick wit, my charming smile, or my dashing good looks. Perhaps it is my ATM card. No matter, they wel-come me there with a hearty handshake and heartfelt how-do-you-do. And a happy face sticker. I roamed the aisles in my quest for needed things, forcefully grasping the oily handle of my errant cart, pushing it hardly in a brave yet vain attempt to keep it veerless. As you shall see, two of those words will play an important part in this narrative: "hardly" and "brave".

Jack stopped typing. He squinted at the screen and grimaced, reading back what he had just written. Not exactly what he had in mind when he found himself starting a blog, but what the hell. A start is a start.

Jack Spurling, self-employed software developer, never seemed to really know what he was getting himself into. For most of his 37 years, things just happened for and to Jack, and his response was invariably to either just roll with the punches or ex-ploit the situation, depending on the circumstances. That's basi-cally how he came to start this blog thing; not that he had any overwhelming desire to share his daily existence with the world, or that the world had any interest in him sharing his daily existence with them, but rather because he was reading someone else's blog, and accidentally hit the "Get Your Own Blog" button. As usual, Jack's response had been "what the hell". He returned to his typing.

> My goal, such as it was, was simple; acquire some milk, cheese, a loaf of bread, and my arch nemesis: fruit. The milk came easily enough, giving me little or no trouble as I snatched it mercilessly from its glassy cavern. The cheese was similarly a pushover, yielding easily to my voracious grasp. The loaf of bread was a piece of cake. This of course proved problematic, since I didn't *want* a piece of cake, I wanted a loaf of bread. But, after weighing my options (it turns out it was really a pound cake), I let it slide. Then I picked it up off the ground where it had slid and put it in my cart.

> That left the fruit. Which, in retrospect, is what I should have done. But dammit, I was there for a *purpose*. I couldn't just go slinking off without the fruit I so desperately desired. That would leave me, like the rest of my life, fruitless. And who was I to scoff at the venerable "Food Pyramid", which insisted that I eat three to four helpings of fruit each and every day, regardless of race, creed, color, or gender? No, fruit *must* be had, and by golly, I was gonna have it.

Jack thought he was funny. But, unlike most people who think they are funny, Jack actually *was* funny. So starting a blog seemed like a natural way for him to let other people in on just how funny he could be. Sure, his friends and coworkers knew he could make them laugh, but there was a wider world out there, and Jack figured this could be a good way to tap into it. Always room for more in the audience, Jack told himself. Accidentally hitting a button to create a blog was a serendipitous accident, but one that almost seemed to him as if it was meant to be…almost as if it were preordained.

> I maneuvered my seemingly drunk cart towards the Fruit and Vegetable section of the B&G. Should I make a full frontal assault, rushing forward with a mad gleam in my eye, waving a plastic bag like a flag and emitting a full-throated Rebel Yell? Or should I be more stealthy, sneaking in from behind the Alcohol and Spirits aisle, removing my shoes so my sneakers would not give me away as they unceremoniously squeaked on the polished linoleum floor? I finally settled on a middle approach…walking slowly yet unabashedly directly into the heart of the section, whistling a nondescript tune from my nondescript lips.

> It is said that there are two types of mistakes one can make in battle: strategic and tactical. It is with no great sense of honor that I must admit I made *both* types of mistake in this campaign. My strategic mistake was one of lack of planning; I had entered the battlefield without a clear purpose in mind, stripping myself of the advantage of a clear goal and a pointed target – I did not know what type of fruit I wanted. My tactical mistake was one of point of entry – I had inadvertently entered the battle zone closer to the vegetables than to the fruits.

Where the hell is this going?

Jack didn't write from personal experience, he didn't write from a moral standpoint or to propagate a particular view, he wrote for *fun*. His sole purpose was to exercise his sense of humor, see what sorts of interesting phrases and comedic predicaments he could muster up out of sheer nothingness. There was no reality behind his musings, and certainly no wish for his words to be prophetic or harbingers of things to come. All he wanted was to be funny.

Slowly, I spun around. Bins of potatoes to my left, lettuce and leafy vegetables to my right, and radishes in my rear. Perhaps I should rephrase that. Or perhaps it's just too late, since you undoubtedly have already formed your mental image, and are undeniably scarred for life. Sorry. Anyway, there was no turniping back now. (C'mon, you didn't think I was going to get through this whole thing without at least *one* really bad fruit-and-vegetable pun, now did you?)

I had to think fast. There was no time to lose, and I *had* to decide what my quarry was. Apples were the obvious choice, but perhaps a bit *too* obvious – it is exactly what they would be expecting. Bananas leapt to mind, and they definitely had a certain appeal (make that *two* really bad fruit-and-vegetable puns), but they were just *too* loaded with potassiumy goodness. No, it had to be something more unusual, something unexpected, like…*papaya!* That's *it!* Papaya are tasty, colorful (in a yellowish amber way), and every other letter is an "a"! Not only *that*, but the plural form of the word is the same as the singular (one papaya, two papaya)…what could be better? I sauntered nonchalantly (question to self: is it even possible to saunter chalantly?) toward the Exotic Fruits display. Carefully, carefully, ever so carefully, I extended my hand. I even included my arm in the process, giving my reach even greater, uh, reach.

Not daring to look directly at the papaya (man, that word *is* fun to type!), and keeping an ever vigilant eye out for that dastardly steward of the section, the Grocery Guy, I surreptitiously grazed my fingers across the smooth surface of the nearest papaya. The cool dry surface responded to my warm caress by remaining actively inert, not daring to release its firm, fleshy, moist insides into an otherwise cold and uncaring world. Put bluntly, I didn't bruise it. But I had to have it; I *had* to enjoy the sweet, sweet deliciousness of this fruit of the tree "Carica papaya", in the genus *Carica*, found originally in the tropical outreaches of Southern Mexico, Central, and South America, though I particularly craved the smaller, sweeter varieties grown in Hawaii. I didn't care that over consumption of its yellowy goodness could cause carotenemia, a harmless yellowing of the soles of the feet and the palms of the hands. None of this mattered; none of this quelled my sudden and burning desire to own this fruit.

Jack had never actually eaten a papaya. He may have encountered bits of it in fruit salads or mixed into other recipes somewhere over the years, but if he had, he was ignorant of this fact. Nevertheless, he seemed to suddenly have an affinity for the fruit, and writing about it became not so much an exercise in absurdity, as an inwardly driven necessity. He couldn't have explained it if he wanted to.

The Grocery Guy wasn't looking. Quick; now was my chance! My hand seized the delicious fruit, and as if it had a mind of its own (my hand, not the delicious fruit, though in fact neither had much of a mental capacity), I stuffed the papaya into my jacket pocket (which was also very sparse in the IQ category). Damn the milk, the cheese, the bread (I mean cake)...none of it mattered; it would just slow me down. I left the rickety grocery cart where it was, a lonely sentinel guarding the path of my escape. The Grocery Guy, damn his potato-like eyes, spotted me making a dash past the Mrs. Dash, and lurched toward me in a vain effort to stop my fleeing-ness.

His effort was to no avail, as I had a head start as well as the quickness of pace that comes from the knowledge that you will soon be a papaya felon. Sweat poured from my brow as I attempted to make good my escape, eyes darting to and fro for (fro for? That's almost as fun to type as papaya!) signs of B&G Supermart Security Personnel. The path was open, the coast was clear, and the automatic door was ajar. I slipped out at a breakneck pace…well, at least at a sprainneck pace, listening intently for the sound of gunshots being fired to impede my illegal departure. I was free, and so was the papaya.

Jack figured that was as good a place to end as anywhere. He really didn't know where else to go with it, but he felt innately that whatever purpose had driven him to write this blog had been appeased, so he called it a night. Maybe, he thought, that will be the end of my blogging career…maybe, he thought, it just isn't for me. But what the hell, Jack could be wrong.

Chapter 2

Jack woke the next morning to the sound of sirens screaming past his second story apartment window. His eyes opened slowly at first, then the realization that the sirens were close by, and not going away, made the sleepiness vanish. He bolted toward the window, and threw up the shade. Across the street, in the parking lot of the B&G Supermart, was a cadre of emergency vehicles. Fire trucks, police cars, paramedics, and an ambulance were all gathered in a huddle in front of the store, their various lights flashing asynchronous with each other, reflecting off the glass doors of the B&G in an illuminated confusion.

Jack threw on some clothes and rushed outside. It wasn't every day so much excitement occurred so close to home, and Jack's curiosity was piqued. What could have caused such a flurry of activity this early? He figured what the hell, he would go find out.

"What's going on, officer?" he asked the first blue uniform he came across, "looks like every civil servant in the city has come to join the party."

The cop was friendly, but terse. "Some guy died in there

this morning. Manager of the produce department."

Jack took a step back in surprise. A slight foreboding shook him for a moment, but it was no match for his curiosity. "What happened? Accident?"

"We don't really know yet. Accident, suicide, murder, who knows? Strangest damn death I've seen in fourteen years on the force, though, I'll tell ya that!"

Jack should have turned around. He should have walked away. He should have gone back to his apartment, locked the door, made himself a pot of coffee, and tried to forget everything about the dead produce manager. But what the hell, curiosity can make you do stupid things, so he stayed.

Jack was unable to get any more information from the cop. He'd said too much already, he claimed, and didn't want to get in trouble. Jack wandered from official to official, asking firefighters, paramedics, and ambulance divers what they knew about this seemingly strange death. Nobody said much of anything, except the ambulance driver. Her only comment was, "I'll be damned if I eat another papaya as long as I live, that's for damn sure."

For the second time that morning, Jack took a step back, only this time the foreboding feeling was not so easily chased off.

"Did you say…*papaya?*" asked Jack.

"Yeah, papaya. You know, those yellow pear-like tropical things. Real sweet, normally, but I doubt this guy enjoyed his." She said it with a half-smile, half-grimace, reveling in her own gallows humor.

Again, however, there was a definite reticence to give more information. Seeing that nobody there was going to be at all forthcoming as to the real cause of death (other than relaying that there was somehow a papaya involved), Jack eventually went back to his apartment. He locked the door, made a pot of coffee, and tried to forget everything about the dead produce manager. But the papaya just didn't let that happen.

Chapter 3

The phone rang.

"Detective Sanderson speaking."

The epitome of the classic burly detective, Sanderson listened intently as the voice on the other end gave him the details. Details he could have done without just before lunch.

"He was *killed*? By a *papaya*?"

Some things just needed repeating. Sanderson had dealt with shootings, stabbings, stranglings, beatings, and a few poisonings. But *never* a papayaing.

"Are you sure?" he asked. This *had* to be a joke. It seemed physically impossible to him that a papaya could do the kind of damage to a human body that was being described to him by the field tech. "It was inserted *where?* Uh huh…right. Wait, there was more than one? Oh, I see, the second one was hard to see because of the swelling, got it. I…I don't even know what to *ask*, this is so weird…"

Sanderson took a deep breath. He had to concentrate just to remember basic protocol, the standard questions that needed to be asked. Somehow, "standard" just didn't seem to apply to this case, and he had only been on it for less than five minutes. It had to get better, right? It just had to. But it didn't.

"Okay, let's see. Name of the victim? Uh huh." He scribbled the details on his notepad.

"And you say he was the manager of the produce department at the B&G Supermart? How long had he worked there? No, not that day, I mean, how long had he been employed?" More scribbling. It was a shame that not even he could read his own notes until his secretary had typed them for him.

"That long, huh? Ok, what time did he arrive…yes, I *know* that's the answer you gave me to the last question, but I'm asking you again…Fine. You have the store manager there? Great. Any known enemies? Wife? Ex? Kids? Domestic Partners? Nothing? Ok, I'll be right down there. Don't let anyone leave, as if I needed to tell you that. And *don't* touch the papaya!"

Sanderson hung up the phone, grabbed his rumpled coat off the back of his chair, and headed out to the car. "Gonna be a looong day," he muttered to himself while waiting for the elevator.

Two hours later, Sanderson was back at his desk. The visit to the scene of the crime had proved fruitless, even if he *had* realized he was making a mental pun. The store manager had no idea why this had happened. No enemies, no apparent motive, and *especially* no idea how a couple of papayas could have ended up embedded in the produce manager like that. Sanderson wondered idly if it had been a quick death, or if papayas caused a lot of pain. Hey, he thought, if he stuttered, it would be papaya pa-pain…like everyone at the scene hadn't already made every conceivable joke. Death by papaya. Best not to dwell on it, he concluded.

Later that evening, Detective Sanderson decided to fire up the old computer and do a little digging on his own time.

The kids were watching a Spongebob Squarepants marathon ("What's that, like, two episodes? Having to watch that crap for half an hour *would* seem like a marathon" he thought.), and Sanderson, though he loved spending quality time with them, just couldn't stomach an evening of Nickelodeon.

Nothing about this case made any sense so far. No suspects, no motive, nothing stolen or broken, and the murder weapon was a tropical fruit. Didn't sound like the Baypoint Killer who had been terrorizing the neighborhood for the past few months – he used a dagger, not a fruit. Not the kind of case that gets you a promotion, he thought, but what it *does* get you is a whole lot of ribbing from the rest of the guys at the station. Well, the only way to shut them up would be to solve the case. And the only way to do *that* would be with good old fashioned, tried and true googling.

Sanderson brought up the search engine on his computer. "B&G Supermart papaya" bought up seventeen matches, most of them useless. But one blog entry…holy crap! It was posted *last night*, and it was for the *same* B&G Supermart where the produce manager had died. The text was just rambling incoherent junk, to Sanderson. But it was all there…the same store, the "Grocery Guy", and the *papaya*…it was all about the *papaya*. Coincidence? How could it be? The detective bookmarked the page, and jotted down the name of the blogger. He could get the address in the morning, no problem – after all, the guy had to live pretty close to the scene of the crime, right? He said so, in the blog.

Chapter 4

Blog Entry Number Two:

Throughout the world of High Tech, no matter what the particular industry or specialty, there is one question that is uttered in every Board Room, every Corner Office, every Cubicle, every hallway. It is a question that sends shivers down the engineers' spines, turns High Paid Marketing Executives into cowering lumps of gelatin, and reduces CEOs to whimpering sniveling toadies. A question so devious in its simplicity, yet so effective in its destruction of time and will, that entire conglomerates have succumbed to its overpowering annihilation. This question is, of course, "Where do you want to go for lunch?"

Don't let this modest question's seemingly innocent candor fool you. Locked within those eight little words is enough raw time-consuming wastefulness to reduce entire corporate divisions to drooling imbeciles. Many a man-year has been utterly wasted in contemplation of this question. On any given day in the United States, with the time spent nationally muttering this phrase and lollygagging around waiting for a decision to be made, one could easily have built the Pyramids of Cheops, the Great Wall of China, or *Lego's* "Star Wars Death Star" model (which has over 3,400 tiny plastic pieces).

But fear not! Salvation is at hand, for here, within the electronic confines of this modest blog, is the solution modern man has been waiting for. I refer, of course, to the Official Guide to Where Do You Want To Go For Lunch (or OGtWDYWTGFL, for short).

Monday

Ah, Monday. The first day of the work week. A blank slate, the entire week spread out before us in all its glory, full of endless possibilities and teeming with potential. A day full of possible problems and potential catastrophes. Usually, Monday is also a traditional "Meeting Day", where large groups of people gather in a common area to attempt nap-ping without being caught. They often are success-ful, as when everyone in a room is trying to nap, they usually aren't awake to catch others doing the same thing. What would make sense as a Lunch Possibility for Monday, you might ask? Or you might not...doesn't matter, I'm gonna answer it an-yway. The OGtWDYWTGFL suggests "Sandwich Shop/Deli" for Monday.

In 1762, John Montagu, fourth Earl of Sandwich, was a gambler. Actually, he was a gambler for pret-ty much most of his life, not just 1762, but 1762 is the year in which we are interested. John gambled and gambled. He loved gambling so much that he hated leaving the gambling tables, even to eat. John Montagu struck upon the brilliant idea of the portable meal – he put a piece of meat between two pieces of bread so he could gamble. The modern day sandwich from a Sandwich Shop is a similar concept, only slightly turned around. Instead of being a piece of meat between two pieces of bread so you can gamble, it is two pieces of bread where you gamble that what is inside is meat.

The specific Sandwich Shop I would recommend for the Monday Midday Repast is "Goto's Deli." Goto's has something for everyone. Meat lovers will revel in the fact that Goto's can shovel more cholesterol onto a six inch bun than the AMA recommends as the average daily consumption of an entire team of Slovakian Shot-putters. For vegetarians, Goto's offers their patented "Bread Sandwiches," the most popular of which is the famous "Whole Wheat on Rye with a side of Pumpernickel." And for our picky eater friends, Goto's offers what must be the blandest entrée ever concocted, a mish-mash of mashed mystery meats spread evenly on a slab of toasted white bread. They call this, for some unknown reason, the Soylent Green Special. Don't ask, just eat.

Jack paused his typing. It seemed incongruous to him to be attempting humor after the morning's tragedy. He didn't know the victim, of course, and although he had been in the B&G Supermart many times, he couldn't picture the produce manager in his mind. But still...he *had* written about the poor guy, albeit indirectly, only last night and even had *papaya* figure prominently in the blog. He felt almost guilty about the whole thing. Nah, that's just being crazy, he scolded himself. How could the one have anything to do with the other? Drop it, forget about it, move on. Back to the blog at hand.

Tuesday

Blog Post Mortem

Tuesday is considered, or should be, at least, a day of rest. Monday is always so hectic, you need a little down-time to recover before hump-day. So Tuesday's meal should be a relaxed, sit-down, full-service dining experience. Despite that, Tuesday's recommendation is Wing's Chinese Restaurant.

Walk into Wing's, and the first thing that happens is the proprietor (presumably Mr. Wing) yells across the restaurant at you completely unintelligibly, gesticulating wildly towards a small, cramped table in the corner. The fact that you are in a party of six, the table seats four, and the restaurant is otherwise empty, is apparently inconsequential. He grabs two chairs from the large, spacious round table by the scenic window (the *empty* large, spacious round table by the scenic window, mind you) and places them diagonally at the corners of the table he is bound and determined to squeeze you in to. His will being stronger than yours, you comply.

There are seventy three "Lunch Specials" on Wing's menu. Each one an inspired concoction specifically designed by Mr. Wing himself to delight and tantalize the discerning palate. Unfortunately, Mr. Wing is not a creative man, so all seventy three menu items consist of chicken parts, soy sauce, and rice. But they *do* have individual, unique and romantic sounding names, such as "Delightful Chicken over Rice", "Chicken over Delightful Rice", and (my personal favorite) "Delightful Chicken Delightfully spread Over Delightful Rice With Delightfully Delightful Soy Sauce Of Delight." It is, in a word, delightful.

Wednesday

Wednesday, in popular parlance, is Hump-Day.

What do you think of when you think of humps? No, not that, keep it clean. You think of camels. And where do you associate with camels? I mean, not "where do you go to associate with camels," that would be kind of sick, and it would be at the zoo. No, I mean, "what part of the world do you think of when you think of camels?" The answer there, of course, is the Middle East. So, what food do you think would be most appropriate for Wednesday? Right...Thai Food! Hey, I've never been very good at geography.

The Thai Palace is not a real palace, just so you know. But it *does* feature some of the best Thai food for several blocks around. Of course, just because it is nestled in the middle of a neighborhood known as "Little Tijuana" doesn't diminish that claim at all. Much. Thai Palace specializes in "Pad Thai", a traditional Americanized doppelganger of a classic Thai dish. It consists of a plate of washed, boiled, and sliced rubber bands (ok, ok, they are noodles...but they *are* kinda rubbery...and they hold newspapers shut pretty well), stir fried with an assortment of fresh garden vegetables (by the way, what vegetables *aren't* garden vegetables? Is there some sort of gigantic mutant vegetable that *wouldn't* fit into a garden?), and topped with a savory peanut sauce. That's right...mix one cup water with one cup Skippy, stir until smooth(er), slop onto Thai food. Of course, the fact that the décor at the Thai Palace consists mainly of statuary elephants in tiaras should clue you in on the peanut sauce. Added bonus: Thai Palace issues you a little card when you dine there, and punches a hole into it every subsequent time you partake of a meal there. When you reach twenty punched holes, you are rewarded with a special treat: they use *crunchy*

Blog Post Mortem

Skippy for the peanut sauce! Woo hoooo!

It was getting late, and Jack had had a long day. Time to call it quits for the night – there would be more time for blogging tomorrow. But…well, he had come *this* far, why not keep going? There were a dozen reasons to stop, actually, but for some reason Jack didn't feel like stopping; he had to keep going.

Thursday

For the last two days, we have been experiencing Ethnic foods. Exotic, unusual, and mostly unidentifiable. But today, Thursday, we are going to step back into an American indigenous form of food, something born and bred in the great Heartland of our country, whose flavors hearken back to the golden days of yesteryear when life was simpler and the foods were unrefrigerated. Yes, that's right friends, today we are going for Italian food!

Mama Sarducci's Ristorante is a tradition in this town. So is Mama Sarducci, but that is another story. But just ask any native (native being anyone who has lived here more than three years) about Mama Sarducci's meatballs, and they will tell you that they are real gems; small, hard, and able to cut glass. And her pasta! Well! All I can say is that it is no coincidence that there is only one letter difference between the words "pasta" and "paste"! This is food that will stick to your ribs. And fingers. And cleave to your esophagus. And wrap itself permanently in unsightly bulges around your torso.

The pizza (for what is a Ristorante without pizza? Other than classy, of course?) is to die for. And for those that have tried it, may they rest in peace. The crust lives up to its name, the sauce is sufficiently reddish in color, and the toppings are spread heavily and uniformly across the entire Ristorante (Mama has a bit of a vision problem). The pizza is then slow oven roasted, though I realize it is not nice to make fun of an oven just because it is slow. Finally, the pizza is removed from the oven, checked for doneness, the head is scratched because the pizza is raw, the light bulb goes on over the head, the oven is turned *on* this time, the pizza is reinserted into the oven, and the actual baking occurs. Once the pizza is really and truly and finally finished, Mama will present you with the pizza, and ask you, in her charming and pleasant old world Irish brogue, if you would like it cut into eight slices, or twelve slices. In an attempt to insert a really old, bad joke into this blog, you will of course answer, "Better cut it into eight slices, I don't think I could eat twelve."

Friday

TGIF. Many people mistakenly believe this to mean "Thank God It's Friday!" We, of course, know better. TGIF actually stands for "Total Gastro-Intestinal Fallout." This is because on Fridays, we suggest none other than Pedro's Authentic Mexican Cantina. There is a good reason Pedro's Authentic Mexican Cantina is called "Pedro's Authentic Mexican Cantina." First off, it is owned by a fellow named Pedro. Secondly, everything in Pedro's is Authentic. The tables are authentic Mexican tables, made in China. The chairs are authentic Mexican chairs, made in sweat shops. The busboys are authentic Mexican busboys, and the waitresses are authentic Mexican waitresses made in Mexico. Even the velvet paintings of Elvis hanging on the authentic walls were authentically purchased in Tijuana. Thirdly, it is a Mexican restaurant, and they really needed to get the word "Mexican" into the name, otherwise it would just be "Pedro's Authentic Cantina", and who could ever possibly guess that it would be a Mexican food establishment with a name like that? And finally, "Cantina", because one of the original waitresses was found stealing from the cash register, so they had to can her...naturally, her name was Tina.

The food at Pedro's is passable. In fact, it is very *quickly* passable; you can pass a Pedro's burrito in no time flat. Pedro doesn't charge much for his burritos, but Pedro had the business savvy, financial acumen, and customer oriented foresight to install pay toilets. Pedro is a rich man.

"Wow, long blog entry," Jack muttered to himself as he shut down his computer for the evening. He was at a loss to explain why he had written it. Sure, he told himself, he wrote for *fun*. To be *funny*. But there was something else, something more pressing, that Jack couldn't quite put his finger on. But he was tired. Exhausted, in fact. And he had no energy to try psychoanalyzing his own motives and driving forces. Such questions would have to wait for another time, but for now, Jack was going to get some sleep.

Chapter 5

Jack was woken the next morning by the sound of the phone ringing. He sat bolt upright in bed, a sense of panic stealing through him. It took a moment for him to get his bearings, realize where he was and recognize the sound that woke him as "phone ringing." He reached across to the bed-side table, and picked up the receiver.

"Uh, h'llo?"

"Mr. Jack Spurling?" the gruff voice at the other end asked.

"Yeah, that's me. Who is this?"

"My name is Detective Sanderson. I'm investigating an incident that I really don't want to get into over the phone. However, your name has come up in conjunction with this case, and I would like to ask you a few questions."

"Crap," thought Jack, unfortunately out loud. "Uh, I mean, uh, sure, I guess…really, I have no clue what this is all about, am I in trouble for something?"

"No, sir, we just have some questions that maybe you can help clarify. I really can't go into any more than that right now. Is it possible for you to come down to the station, and we can talk face to face?"

"I guess, yeah. I, uh, just woke up, so give me an hour to shower and shave and throw some clothes on…"

"No problem, sir, take your time. I assume you know where the station is? Just ask for me, Detective Sanderson, at the front desk. I'll leave word there that I'm expecting you."

"Ok, I guess. Ummm…see ya soon?" Jack hung up the phone.

"Crap" he reiterated.

An hour and a half later, Jack Spurling was seated in Detective Sanderson's office.

"So, Detective, mind telling me what this is all about? I'm really quite confused by it all, and more than a little nervous…I've never been interviewed by a detective before."

"Sure, Mr. Spurling. Mind if I call you Jack? No? Good. Anyway, Jack, there was a death across the street from you yesterday; the produce manager at the B&G Supermart. I was wondering if you had any information that might be useful to us in our investigation."

Jack was getting a little sweaty. He couldn't help it, he got that way when he was nervous. He was tempted to just lie, pretend he knew nothing, not even that there was a death. But he also knew he would probably be caught if he tried that – he had asked too many questions yesterday, too many people had seen him. And perhaps to them, he had seemed a little *too* interested…maybe that was why he was here.

"Yeah, I, uh, heard about that…" Jack decided maybe a bit of truth here would be the best way to go. Not *all* the truth, of course. How could he explain the really strange coincidence of his blog? But as for the rest, he'd better fess up.

"The sirens woke me up, I looked out the window, and saw all the hubbub going on at the B&G. I have to confess, I was really curious. Who wouldn't be? So I went over there to see what was going on."

"Uh huh." The detective grunted, in a very unconvincing manner. "Did you see anyone go in or out *before* that? Anyone suspicious hanging around the Supermart? After all, you *do* have a view of the place from your window, don't you?"

They know where I live, obviously, thought Jack. Wonder what else they know. And, come to think of it, he *hadn't* given his name to anyone yesterday when he was asking all those questions, poking around. How had this guy gotten his phone number? A panicked feeling started creeping up Jack's spine; anxiety started getting the best of him. I wonder if...no they couldn't. How could they have seen the blog? Why would they have been reading that thing? It didn't make any sense. Except...Jack was a programmer. He was used to looking at problems from a lot of different angles, trying to find solutions by thinking outside the proverbial box. Maybe, reasoned Jack, it *does* make sense that they would have read his blog. They couldn't have come across it randomly, he reasoned, the odds against that were astronomical. So how *else* would one stumble across a blog? Well, when he wanted to read about something he was interested in, he would do a search on the internet, and invariably there were blog entries mixed in with the other search results. So...if Sanderson wanted to research the B&G Supermart, he would do an online search. But if he threw in a few other keywords, like...papaya! Of *course* Jack's blog entry would probably pop right to the top! How many matches could there *be*? So, Sanderson knew about the blog; he had to, it was the only reason for Jack's being here that made any sense. What should he do? The only thing he *could* do was, again, tell the truth. It wasn't like he *did* anything bad, actually. He just wrote a stupid *blog* entry that *happened* to coincidentally have some words in common with Sanderson's case.

"Uh, Detective Sanderson, I think I should tell you, that I, uh, well, I write a blog, see? And it just so happens, *completely* by accident, I mean like a *total* coincidence, that I made up this story in my blog the other night about the B&G Supermart. In fact, and this is what really blows me away, it's so weird, freaky *Twilight Zone* kinda stuff, but I, uh talked about a papaya. I mean, the guy, the manager there, *his* death had something to do with a papaya, right? That's what they told me in the parking lot yesterday, anyway, and I would have no reason to doubt them. So that's kinda freaking me out, ya know? That I would write this totally made-up story, and stuff from it shows up in real life the next day."

Jack stopped there, took a deep breath, and looked at the detective, waiting for a response. Sanderson sat there for a moment, drumming his meaty fingers on his desk, formulating a response to this rambling, nearly incoherent "confession" of writing a blog.

"Yeah, Jack. I've read it. That's how I knew I needed to call you."

Jack felt a small internal thrill, knowing that he had guessed right about how the detective discovered him.

"The problem I see with it, though, Jack, is that it is just a bit *too* coincidental, ya know? I mean, a *papaya*? Really, what are the odds you would write that *the night before* an incident like that took place. I hate to say it, Jack, but that's *very* suspicious to me." The detective reasoned.

"I agree, detective. If I were you, I would be suspicious too. But you gotta believe me, as weird as it sounds, it *was* a coincidence."

"Well, Jack, we aren't going to arrest you right now, so

don't worry. If I were to take you to trial and all I had was this 'coincidence', as strange as it is, they would laugh me out of the courthouse. I'll be honest with you, we *have* no other evidence tying you to the crime…no fingerprints, no witnesses, not even a shade of a motive. Nothing. So, for now at least, you are simply considered a 'person of interest'."

Jack was about to get up to leave; the detective motioned him to wait a moment.

"Hold up, Jack. Let's look at that blog one more time, shall we? Just to see if maybe there is something there I missed the first time. Maybe you could explain to me what you were thinking while you were writing it." The detective swiveled around and punched in a few keys on his computer. "I have your blog bookmarked, I…oh, I see you have added a new entry! I gotta say, I find your stuff pretty funny. Hold on; mind if I read through it for a minute?"

Jack sat there nervously, as the detective read through the blog. It was disconcerting, he thought, that he was almost more nervous about whether detective Sanderson would find this entry *funny*, as he was about being a suspect for murder. The detective chortled and snickered every few moments, as Jack sat on pins and needles. Five minutes later, just as the detective was getting to the end of the "Friday" entry on the blog, the phone rang.

"Sanderson here…yeah? Another one…who…*What?* You're *kidding* me! Gimme that name again…when did this happen?… Twenty minutes ago, why…but that's impossible! Hold on, let me call you back."

The detective's normally ruddy face was ashen, as he turned and stared at Jack. He must have stared at Jack for a full minute, making Jack's feeling of panic progress into a barely-suppressed hysteria. What happened? What was going on?

"I don't know how to say this, Jack, I can't make heads or tails of it. But apparently, around twenty minutes ago, Mr. Wing from Wing's Chinese Restaurant died. Chopstick, right into the heart. You know, Mr. Wing? The guy you talked about in this blog entry?"

Jack almost fainted. This just couldn't be happening, it was inconceivable.

"But, I...I didn't...but..." Jack stammered.

"Don't worry, Jack. We know it wasn't you. His wife was with him at the time, claims it was an accident. He was scurrying around that small kitchen at his restaurant when he tripped and fell, impaling himself on a plastic chopstick. They called *me* because they want to make sure the *wife* didn't have any part in this, uh 'accident'".

Relief instantly swept over Jack, but was almost immediately followed by a sense of dread. How could this have happened? *Again?* He had been in Wing's restaurant a dozen times or so, but no more or no less than any of the other restaurants he frequented. He knew Wing by sight, but that was about it. Why had he bothered to write about him last night? Seemed like he was just "going along with it", his blog rambling on where it may. Same with the whole B&G thing...no particular reason for writing it, just...what the hell! It seemed funny at the time.

*   *   *   *   *

Detective Sanderson was shaken. He supposed it was *possible* that Jack was in collusion with Wing's wife, but that was just so preposterous, he didn't give it much credence. After all, if Jack *did* have something to do with it, *why* would he have written about it in a blog? Same with the B&G Super-mart thing, come to think of it. Plus, the most convincing thing to Sanderson, was his gut instinct. All his years on the force had taught him how to read people, and Sanderson was convinced that Jack was just as confused and perplexed by all of this as he was. But, on the other hand…how could this be mere coincidence? The odds were off the charts.

"Okay, Jack, you're free to go."

"That's it?" asked Jack, "You're not going to charge me or something?"

"Nah, I don't believe you had anything to do with these incidents. You seem like an honest enough guy, and I don't really have anything else to go on. I believe you. But just the same, do me a favor and don't leave town for a few days, okay?"

"No problem. I have nowhere I was supposed to go…and I do all my computer consulting work from my home office, so I have no business trips or anything planned."

"Oh, and Jack…keep up the good work on the blog. It's really quite funny!"

Chapter 6

That evening, Jack decided *not* to write a blog entry. He was just too creeped out by the occurrences of the last few days. He didn't really *believe* there was any correlation between his funny blog and the horrendous events that had happened. But still, why tempt fate? He decided to take a break for a few days; besides, it was hard to be funny with the memories of those two deaths hanging around in his head. Jack powered down his laptop and shut the lid, grabbed a beer from the fridge, and sat down in front of the TV.

Click. Nightime soap opera, yuck. Click. Ugh, I hated that movie. Click. More game shows. Click. Click. Click. Click click click click click click click click click click. Nothing. Jack couldn't concentrate. Maybe he could read for a while before bed? Hmmm, don't want funny. And no murder mysteries, thank you very much! Historical fiction? Nah. Nothing sounded good.

His eye fell on his computer. No, he thought, I told myself not tonight. I just don't feel like it. But as much as he told himself he didn't feel like it, he did. He very much wanted to do a bit of writing. And no matter what he did or tried to do that evening, he inevitably gravitated toward the computer. Until finally…what the hell, nothing else to do.

Blog Entry Number Three:

Ever notice how companies are always putting out press releases about the most simple of things? Self-serving awards, internal promotions, and partnerships with other companies that are nothing more than a way of *two* companies putting out a press release instead of one? I never noticed it either. But now that you mention it…

What would happen if they took it to the next level, and put out massive press announcements over truly miniscule and mundane occurrences?

For Immediate Release

February 31, 2016

Mike Brooklyn Still Employed at Coastline Networks

Coastline Networks, Inc, the industry leader in Converged Networking (whatever the hell that means) announced today that self-proclaimed engineer Mike Brooklyn has been continuously employed in the Coastline West Coast(line) Division for over two and a half years. "We never thought it would get this far," said Daniel G. Norman, President and Chief Executive Officer of Coastline Networks, "because we figured he was good for two, maybe three months tops before he flaked out. But we feel that we, as a company, have gone above and beyond the customary and normal in our industry by allowing such a worthless individual to ride on the coattails of others' success for such an extended period of time. We are very proud of this accomplishment."

Brooklyn's actual contributions, from a "work per-
formed" standpoint over the twenty eight months,
have amounted to little more than sharpening a few
pencils, cleaning his whiteboard, and using a signif-
icant amount of Corporate internet bandwidth.
Many in the Industry feel that this may be overstat-
ing his output, though, since most of the pencils
sharpened in the high-speed electric pencil sharp-
ener were in fact mechanical pencils. Insiders are
quick to point out that Brooklyn's whiteboard cleaning skills are second to none, as he uses a unique
and proprietary combination of ammonia-based
cleaners, natural citrus enhanced enzymes, and
spit. Insiders are also just as quick to point out that
they wouldn't be caught dead borrowing his whiteboard eraser.

But by far Brooklyn's most valued accomplish-
ments, at least to himself, have come in the area of
non-work related goofing off. Brooklyn has cultivat-
ed a keen sense of when Management is looking,
and has used this innate skill to his advantage. Often Brooklyn will switch to a Microsoft Excel
spreadsheet on his computer screen mere moments before his supervisor enters his cubicle, thus
hiding the pirated movie downloads in progress. He
has the uncanny ability to talk into his iPod while
listening to illegally obtained music, in an attempt to
make it look like he is on a cell phone. And his use
of the Corporate Coffee Pot, in terms of both fre-
quency and volume, is second to none.

When asked why Coastline Networks Inc. doesn't
just relieve Mr. Brooklyn of his employment status,
Mr. Norman responds, "Well, it isn't all that easy,
really. We hired him under a federally mandated

government program known as "No Idiot Left Behind". It would be both a federal offense, and an extreme waste of huge bloated government subsidies paid to us in large brown paper bags to fire Mr. Brooklyn. Besides, nobody can sniff out the really *good* porn on the internet like he can! You're not writing this down, are you?"

Questions and inquiries regarding Mr. Brooklyn's employment can be directed to:

Jane Doe. Really. I swear.

Director of Human Suffering...er...Services

Coastline Networks Incorporated

Really Stupid Press Release Division

--##--

Jack hit the "Submit" button on the blog, checked to make sure it was sent successfully, and powered down for the second time that evening. "No problems here," he thought to himself, "I totally made this up...Coastline, Brooklyn, Norman...not a single real person or place in the whole blog."

Jack went to bed, and instead of being antsy and agitated, slept a very sound and deep sleep.

Chapter 7

Jack was almost not surprised when the phone rang in the morning, waking him up. This was getting to be a regular occurrence he mused as he wiped the sleep from his eyes and picked up the receiver.

"H'llo?"

"Jack. Detective Sanderson here."

"Oh, good morning, detective? What can I do for you?"

"Jack, what the hell is going on here? I read your blog this morning, more from a desire to have a chuckle than any official reason, when I read what you wrote about Coastline."

"Did you like it? I kinda liked the concept of the Trivial Press Release, myself…"

"Jack! Don't tell me you didn't hear? About Coastline Precision Machining? It's all over the news."

"Huh? What's Coastline Precision Machining? I just made that company and all those names up. What are you talking about?"

"A few minutes ago, I got the official report. It seems like a guy down at some place called Coastline Precision Machining, down by the docks, got fed up with his boss and plugged him a few rounds with a forty-five."

"What? No way. How can that…I made Coastline up. Besides, the blog wasn't about a shooting…"

"Jack, listen to me. Listen carefully. The shooter's name was Mike Queens. The boss, the guy he shot…was Dan Saxon."

It took Jack a few moments for it to sink in. What were the names he used? Oh yeah. Mike Brooklyn, and Dan Norman. Brooklyn…Queens. Norman…Saxon.

Jack dropped the receiver and slumped back onto the bed. It couldn't be…it just *couldn't*.

"Jack? Jack? You there? Hello???"

Chapter 8

Best to just ignore it, to not think about it. Really, it was all just a bunch of really freaky coincidences. There is no way, Jack thought, that *any* of this could be related in any way to his blog. It was beyond the realm of comprehension, it wasn't worth thinking about.

Jack went about his daily business in as normal a fashion as he could. There were a few adjustments he made, however. For instance, on his computer his Home Page was usually "Yahoo News". But it seemed like the attack at Coastline Precision Machining was being picked up by every news service out there, and Jack really didn't want to hear any more about it. So, today his home page was "The Onion". Also, Jack frequently listened to the local Talk Radio station while he worked. But not today; a local homicide was naturally a topic of discussion. Not exactly the hype of the Baypoint Killer, but certainly better than local politics.

Jack buried himself in his work. After all, as a programmer, he could easily slip into the digital world of logic, and submerse himself for hours with the raw concentration necessary to solve a difficult problem. He needn't come up into the real world, the world where employees plugged their bosses, Chinese chefs impaled themselves on chopsticks, and produce managers…well, actually, Jack didn't *know* exactly what happened to the produce manager with the papaya. But whatever it was, it wasn't pretty, and Jack avoided that world for as long as possible. He worked straight through his usual lunch time and well into the evening; a coding marathon.

But eventually, Jack had to emerge. He'd gotten about as far on the job project as he could in one sitting, and needed a break. Besides, he was hungry, and really needed to use the bathroom. Too many factors to ignore there, so Jack had to leave his Digital Fortress of Solitude and come up, kicking and screaming, into the harsh light of reality. He carefully saved his work, pressed the power key on the laptop to power down, and shut the lid with a satisfying click. He was not going to open it up again until tomorrow, period.

After taking care of his more pressing business, Jack rummaged through the fridge…nothing; at least, nothing that didn't have either a layer of "hair" growing on it or an expiration date of last year, or both. Jack knew he had to go to the store and pick up some groceries. The thought sent a shiver up his spine. Go…to the B&G Supermart? No way. Too unnerving. Too raw still. Yeah, yeah, he told himself, so stuff happened there, so what? *You* know you had nothing to do with it, so what's the problem? Jack spent a good ten minutes trying to convince himself that going to the B&G was no big deal. He even Triple Dog Dared himself, knowing full well that no self-respecting male on the planet could possibly pass by a challenge like that. Apparently, Jack was not a self-respecting male. In the end, Jack completely convinced himself that what he was in the mood for was pizza delivery.

Thirty minutes. That was the guaranteed delivery time.

Jack waited nervously, unwilling to turn on the TV on the chance (a good one) that the Coastline Precision Machining story would pop up. He fidgeted with the remote. He set it down. Fifteen seconds later, he picked it back up. He kept glancing over at his computer. He wanted to do a little research for his next blog...er, no. Not for the blog, for the work project he was working on. Yeah, forget about that stupid blog, who needed it? Not worth the aggravation, that's for sure. Never again, no sir, you wouldn't find Jack doing any more blogging. What would be the point, Jack thought? It's not like he got *paid* to do it, or it was even something he could put on a resume. And as far as he knew, the only person who read the damn thing was Detective Sanderson.

Five more minutes went by. Jack got up, wandered over to the computer desk, and sat down on the swivel chair at his desk. He told himself that this was the most comfortable chair in the house. That's why he wanted to sit there. That's all, merely for the comfort. What a great chair, so cushy, and the wheels let you roll around wherever you needed to be. Yep, this is the best chair to sit on. Jack had no intention of opening his computer, though, no way. Just because he was sitting right next to it didn't mean he was going to succumb to the temptation.

Jack's mind conveniently wandered back to a problem he was having with the program he was developing. Hmmm, maybe a quick Google search would help him come up with some potential solutions. It was worth a shot. But of course, he had promised himself that he wouldn't turn on his computer. Although...really, this was different, right? This was for *work*, and he had made that promise specifically so he wouldn't do any blogging, and he *wasn't* going to blog, he just wanted to look something up on Google, and this was for his *job*, for Chrissake, and wasn't that more important than some stupid old promise he had made himself over a stupid superstitious feeling which was just dumb? Jack opened the laptop and powered it up.

Five minutes later, Jack was poring over the several hundred Google results his search had come up with. He was keeping to his promise, at least to the intent if not the letter, and hadn't come anywhere near logging into his blog account. But there were too many options, he had to narrow his search down...Googling was a fine art, and it took a lot of practice to find *just* the right combination of keywords to get you what you really wanted. But first...Jack stretched, got up from his comfortable chair, and went to the fridge for a beer. At least *those* he still had in stock!

After fumbling around in the refrigerator for a few minutes and finding what he was looking for, Jack ambled back to his desk, plopped down on the comfortable chair, and swiveled around to face the screen of his computer. Jack froze when he saw the screen. The beer slipped from his weakened grasp, and fell crashing to the floor; Jack didn't even notice. He held his breath, and didn't move...he couldn't move. All he could do is stare in confusion and dread. There in front of him, the cursor blinking as if to beckon him, was the entry screen for Jack's blog.

Chapter 9

Blog Entry Number Four:

The year was 2984, and Spaceman Spliff was on a Mission. He had been named after an ancient god, whose various other names included Lord Ganja, Holy Hemp, and Mary Jane (as chronicled in the Holy Book of the Great and Foolish Dead). Spliff didn't know much about the Mission; it was Double-Top-Secret, and he wouldn't find out the details until several months after Mission Completion. Not that he would *know* when the Mission was completed, of course. The only information that had been given him was that he was to take his Spacecraft, "Craft of Space", to the far reaches of the Galaxy, to a planet called Zorg (because *all* Galaxies, by Law, must have a planet called Zorg), in an attempt to undo the Wrongs that had been done against the Noble and Honest citizens. Hey, that's what it said in the Mission Dossier; don't blame *him* if it sounded a bit cloyingly altruistic.

Jack wasn't exactly sure how it had happened... things were a bit sketchy in his mind – it was all done in kind of a fog. The last *clear* memory he had was the shock of seeing the Blog screen on his computer. There was *no way* he had left it there. He had been very careful *not* to go to that page. It was all some sort of a fluke; a mistake. Sometimes the cursor on his machine just floated across the screen by itself. Maybe it was something along those lines, where some glitch had just, by itself, clicked on the shortcut icon for his Blogger page. That *must* be it; there was no other explanation.

But *after* he saw it, well, he didn't know why he didn't just close the window. It would have been easy enough, but he couldn't. Literally could not. His brain told his hand to move the mouse to the little "x" in the upper right corner of the page, but the hand refused. The hand instead clicked on the "New Entry" button. Jack watched as it happened, dazed, confused, and almost as if he was a remote person watching what was going on, and not the actual person doing the clicking. Then the typing started. "Blog Entry Number Four" was typed completely out of his control, or so it seemed. After that, he seemed to start to come out of the stupor, slowly, and take control of his actions. Although, "control" didn't really explain it. He couldn't close the window, he couldn't shut the computer, he couldn't walk away. It wasn't as if he were physically restrained, but no matter how much his mind begged and pleaded, his body just didn't comply with any of these requests. But he *did* have control, *complete* control, over *what* he typed.

Jack was a natural born skeptic. He was still absolutely convinced that a whole series of strange coincidences had been plaguing him; but that's all that it was; coincidence. Still, what the hell…why take any unnecessary chances. Jack decided to *not* write about anybody that could be affected, to not mention *any* real or possibly real people or events. A made-up character, set in the distant future, would be a safe choice. He even resisted the urge to name the protagonist after his favorite cartoon strip alter-ego, and settled for something not-quite-the-same, just to be sure. He may not be able to prevent himself from writing, but Jack could still eliminate any chance of accident.

> Spliff checked the fuel gauge. He had enough diplonium in the tanks to get him all the way to Zarkon Beta and back, if necessary! His frabulator was fully charged, his xenitractor cocked and ready, and even his perblumious snarfer was up to the task ahead. In short, Spliff was ready. As ready as a flumious granjeb at a flark station.

Jack wanted to stop at this point. He thought maybe he had done enough to ease the pressure thrust upon him to blog. But somehow, he couldn't pull himself away from the keyboard. Just wasn't possible. The only option left to Jack was to keep typing…keep typing…

> Spliff fired up "Craft of Space" and headed spaceward. It was a long and tiresome journey, and his only respite from the overpowering ennui was the occasional game of "Jipbits" against the onboard computer. "Jip," called out Spliff to the computer, as he cornered his opponent's Bitblat for the fourth time running, "I can't believe you fell for the Travastian Gambit again! Will you never learn?" Suddenly, he felt a tremendous jerk (the proper form of the noun, not the slang), and the Jipbits pieces went scattering all over the cockpit. "What the…" but before Spliff could complete his epithet, he saw through the Visifore Screen what had caused the sudden stop. The "Craft of Space" had somehow run smack dab into the starboard aft appendage of

an Intergalactic Frizzlehopper!

pause for dramatic effect

Now, as everyone knows, an Intergalactic Frizzle-hopper is *not* something with which to trifle. They can be mean, cantankerous, and just plain sploogy. A sploogy Frizzlehopper was not what Spliff need-ed now; the good people of Zarkon Beta were counting on him! Spliff grabbed the controls of the xenitractor, and with the care and precision that on-ly comes to those in the Space Corps after long years of practice, he guided the device towards the Frizzlehopper's duoplenum. "Got ya now," thought Spliff, trigger finger slowly squeezing the controls, "say bye to your duoplenum!" With a quick burst of bright energy, the Frizzlehopper suddenly found it-self tumbling wildly through the void of space, una-ble to control its course without its trusted duople-num.

Without warning, Jack quickly shut the lid on his laptop, and pushed his chair back from the desk. He sat silently for a moment, waiting. His hands hung limply by his side; he dared not move. The only thing he heard was the magnified sound of his own breathing. A minute passed. Then two. He felt apprehension, true, but no panic. No overwhelming desire or need to go back to the computer. Was that it? Was he done, at least for now? He continued to wait, too scared to move away lest the undeniable impulse he had faced earlier forced him back to the keyboard. After ten minutes, he finally went to bed. But he didn't sleep very well that night.

Chapter 10

AP News Wire

CAPE CANAVERAL, FL – The country mourns today at the news of another disastrous loss for the Space Shuttle program. Early this morning, the Space Shuttle Discovery, while en route back from a construction mission at the International Space Station, was struck by a large meteorite. All seven astronauts on board were killed instantly in the explosion.

Meteorites are commonly encountered by the Space Shuttles, but most are miniscule and do no damage. According to scientists at the Kennedy Space Center, the odds of a meteorite of this size (approximately 1 meter in diameter) striking the Space Shuttle were astronomical. There is no defense against such a catastrophe.

The seven astronauts on board were pilot Bill Oefelein, mission specialists Bob Curbeam, Nick Patrick, Joan Higginbotham, and Suni Williams, and Commander George "Spiff" Hobson.

Hobson's nickname was based on a comic character named Calvin, created by Bill Watterson, who had an alter-ego named "Spaceman Spiff."

No remains can be recovered, and NASA has little hope of retrieving any pieces of the wreckage from space for analysis. Memorial services will be held next Wednesday. The nation mourns the loss of these brave pioneers.

No no no no no no no no no...Jack read the article again, just to be sure.

Chapter 11

Jack was not surprised by the knocking at the door, nor was he flustered by who it was. He invited the detective in and offered him a seat and a beer. Sanderson accepted the first and passed on the second, but only because he was on duty.

"Jack, I came down here as soon as I read the blog this morning." It was Detective Sanderson. "Are you okay?"

"Okay? *Okay?* What the hell kind of question is that? *Of course* I'm not okay. I just killed seven astronauts! How is that 'okay'?"

"Jack, calm down. You didn't kill them, it was an accident. A wildly improbable accident, but there's no other explanation. It's just a blog, for Chrissake. There are probably a million of them out there, and they can't all be controlling the future or prescient or whatever the hell you think is going on. And what would be so special about yours? Why you, of all people? Nothing personal, but you seem to me to be a pretty normal, average guy."

Sanderson said the words, but Jack could tell from the sound of his voice that he didn't exactly believe them. Jack didn't believe them either. A posting about a papaya death at the B&G Supermart, well, that's strange, but not so far out of the ballpark that you couldn't buy into it. And then the thing with Mr. Wing. Again, really, all there was in the blog was the name "Wing", Jack hadn't really called the death. And the Coastline thing. Well, now it was getting pretty spooky. What were the chances of "making up" the same name? Although, in a shipping town with docks on the waterfront, maybe that wasn't so eerie after all. But having a "Spaceman Spiff" reference, albeit tangential, just before a shuttle catastrophe? Now we're into some seriously bizarre coincidence.

"Look," said Sanderson, "if you're really convinced that this is all some cosmic premonition or something and it is scaring you, then just don't write any more. Simple!"

"You don't understand. I tried. I don't know how to explain it, but there was nothing I could do *but* write the blog. You've seen people with compulsive disorders before, right? Like that detective on TV, Monk? No matter what is going on around him, he *has* to dust the lamp or touch the parking meters in order or whatever…he doesn't have a choice in the matter. It's kinda like that. Everything I did led me back to the computer. I couldn't think straight, couldn't concentrate, couldn't even hardly breathe. Am I making any sense?"

"How about you just unplug the computer, huh?" Sanderson said. "Maybe take some sleeping pills or have a few drinks to relax you before bed? C'mon, this is all crazy…I know it seems totally incredible and all, if you think about it, but maybe it's kinda like horoscopes. You know, people read their horoscope, and they *swear* it is about them. But if you read them *any* sign's horoscope, and *tell* them it's theirs, then they will say the same thing…people read personal connections into all sorts of things. Well, maybe these connections you are seeing is like that...maybe they are just random occurrences that you are making personal connections with. It's not like you *said* "the Space Shuttle will blow up." It's not like you *said* "the produce manager at the B&G Supermart will meet a death by papaya." No, these are just little *bits* of what you wrote, intersecting with little *bits* of reality, in a fashion that, though seemingly eerie, is really just personal perception."

Jack thought about what Sanderson was saying. He was right, of course. He *had* to be. The so-called crossovers with reality were just bits and pieces, fragments really, of what he had written. There must be hundreds of such fragments in any given blog, and it made sense that these fragments could match up with the inestimable number of things and occurrences that happened every day in real life. Yeah, it *seemed* awfully close to being related, but if you thought about the millions of blog entries that were published on the web every day, well, something like this was inevitable. Jack felt a little better, but he couldn't help being a bit upset by the fact that this inevitable occurrence was happening to him.

"Thanks, Sanderson. I appreciate the concern, and I think what you are saying makes a ton of sense. Tell ya what, let me take you out to lunch, my treat. I know a little place just down the block that serves a killer pierogi."

"Talked me into it. Just one favor, though...don't mention me in the same blog entry as 'killer pierogi', alright?"

Chapter 12

Jack felt a lot more at ease that evening. His lunch with the detective had been relaxed and friendly. They talked about all sorts of things; what detective work was like, what sort of cases Sanderson was working on, and lots of cop-on-the-street type stories that had Jack alternately laughing and cringing. Jack in turn had talked about some of the computer projects he had worked on; how he had hit a bit of a jackpot in the tech boom with a web company (now defunct) that had blazed then fizzled, but left Jack with a sizeable chunk of change when all was said and done. About how he, Jack, didn't really need to work right now, but enjoyed the challenge of the consulting work he was doing, and wanted to keep up with technology, "just in case."

By the end of lunch, the two had become friends. Not, perhaps, the sort of deep friendship that can only come with years of camaraderie and shared hardships, but more the sort of friendship one can achieve by several hours of talk and a shared lunchtime. Jack had lost some of the fear and apprehension that the detective had naturally instilled in him, and now looked on him not as a Member of the Police Force, but as just a regular guy. A regular guy that thought Jack's blog entries were pretty darn funny. A regular guy that nearly had Jack convinced that the blog was nothing more than a blog, and that the mind can play terrible tricks on you, especially the creative mind.

Jack was actually able to watch TV that evening. Mostly. Oh, sure he had twinges here and there, itches that made him want to amble over to the computer desk and fire off a few lines. But he was able to hold them at bay. He was actually able to concentrate on the sitcom he usually enjoyed, and even did passably better than the contestants he was watching on "Jeopardy!". A sense of relief settled gently over him, and he was lulled into the belief that tonight he would be unencumbered with his recent compulsion.

Until bedtime, that is. Jack was tired; it had been an emotional day, and wanted to hit the sack. But he kept glancing in the direction of the computer. He brushed his teeth, and thought he heard a "beep" coming from the desk. Nope, just his imagination. He was searching his bookshelf for a book to settle in with, when he thought he heard clicking sounds, like the sound of a keyboard. Again, a quick glance showed him it was his imagination. Just to be sure, he went to his desktop computer, powered it down, and unplugged the cord from the wall. No random sounds should be bothering him now!

Jack heard no further sounds, imaginary or otherwise. He lay in bed reading for a while (Stephen King, probably a bad choice), and when he found himself reading the same sentence three or four times, he closed his book, closed his eyes, and drifted off to sleep.

Two hours later, Jack woke with a start. He went from a deep slumber to immediately being wide awake. He peered around his room, making out the shapes and shadows of his everyday life. Which he shouldn't have been able to do; the room *should* have been pitch dark – the room darkening shades were drawn, no nightlight was on...so why could he see? Dimly, but he could see. He realized there was a faint glow emanating from the next room, from an unknown and unexpected source.

Jack rolled out of his bed, and crept toward the door. He slowly peeked around the door jamb, not knowing what to expect. There, on his desk, was his computer. Plugged in, powered up, screen glowing, throwing a faint blue light throughout the room. As Jack cautiously approached the softly humming machine, his heart skipped as he realized that on the screen was the entry page for his blog, cursor blinking invitingly.

Jack *knew* he had logged off the computer earlier. He *knew* he had shut off the power, and he *knew* he had even gone so far as to unplug the damn machine. This must be a joke, he thought, though he knew full well that it wasn't.

"Sanderson?" he called into the still night air, "Sanderson, you jerk, are you in here? Show yourself! This isn't funny, you know. Not funny at all. Sanderson!"

As the sounds of his increasingly panicky voice were swallowed into the darkness of the night, he realized just how alone he really was. He knew Sanderson wasn't there. This wasn't the kind of joke he would play. But more importantly, Jack knew why the computer was on. Why the computer was at the blog entry screen, waiting. He knew there was no escaping, that he had to write, he had to create yet another blog entry, and, worst of all, that the blog entry would mean disaster for someone, somewhere.

"*No*," he told himself, "I will *not* do it. The hell with it." Jack walked over to the machine, and ripped the cord out of the wall, and the screen immediately went dark with just a pinpoint of bright blue in the center, which faded to nothingness within seconds. He went to the other side of the room, and plopped down into the big easy chair that was there.

I'll just watch it, Jack thought. *I won't succumb, I just won't.*

Fifteen uneventful minutes passed, then fifteen more. At forty five minutes into his vigil, Jack's eyes started getting droopy. Another fifteen minutes went by, and Jack was sound asleep, slumped in his chair. He didn't know how much time had passed when he suddenly startled awake. There, on the desk, glowing invitingly, was his computer. Plugged in, screen glowing, throwing a faint blue light throughout the room.

This time, the compulsion was too great. Jack didn't stand a chance. He stood up and shuffled towards the desk, dragging his feet as if he were a zombie from a cheesy horror flick. He sat in the chair, and slowly lifted his hands up, and rested them on the keyboard. He knew he had to type; there was no denying that whatever was forcing him to do this was not going to let him off the hook. He stared at the blinking cursor, trying to will himself to look away, will himself to stand up and run out of room, out of the building, and anywhere other than here, will himself to pick up the computer and smash it against the wall. He couldn't, though. His will wasn't that strong. With a sigh that reached into the very core of his being, Jack gave in. What the hell...

Blog Entry Number Five:

He walked through the crowded parking lot, pressing the button and waving the car's remote like a priest sprinkling water on a heathen crowd. The high pitched "bleep-bleep" finally told him the general direction of his vehicle. Or, at least, of a vehicle with the same remote as his. Hmmm…sounded like it came from this direction. Press press. Nope, must have been an echo. Weren't echoes usually the product of a large *empty* space? So how come this place was wall to wall vehicles, and still sounded like a, like a…a place with an echo.

Jack was having trouble concentrating. He couldn't blame himself for having this trouble, when he knew that anything he wrote could mean disaster for someone somewhere. That's why he decided that there weren't going to be any people in this blog entry. All the other catastrophes had been based on the people he mentioned in his blog. Maybe, just maybe, if he avoided people altogether, nothing bad would happen…Maybe. He felt he could use a generic "he", that would be safe enough, but *no* other references to people.

"Bleep-bleep." Aha! He swore he saw the subtle flash of the brake lights as they blinked in coordinated unison with the melodic sound of the alarm bleeps. Over there! Sure enough, his car was there, waiting as patiently as a semi-rusted hunk of metal and plastic could wait. Well, the metal part was rusted…the plastic was merely corroded. He walked confidently up to the contraption, and swung the door open with a majestic sweep of his hand. An unfortunate thing to do, seeing as the parking lot was so crowded, and the car next to him was a recent model Cadillac. No matter; he was probably doing the Cadillac owner a favor, anyway, because the owner would not have any trouble finding the vehicle, since its alarm was going full blast in a cacophony of dire claxons. A favor well worth the slight gash in the otherwise pristine white paint of the Cadillac.

He sat in the car and turned the key. This proved to be completely ineffective, until he realized that he had not inserted the key into the ignition, but was just turning it in the air. Once this problem was corrected, he resumed turning the key, and the ancient machine roared to life. A cloud of noxious fumes belched forth from the automobile. "Excuse me," he said to no one in particular, "Indian food does that to me!" The car also emitted a cloud of noxious fumes. The scratch in the Caddy immediately started corroding.

He put the clunker in reverse, looking over his shoulder in much the same way as Carol Brady did in that one episode of the Brady Bunch where she was backing up in that big station wagon of hers in the parking lot at the grocery store and Bobby and Cindy were fighting in the back seat and she accidentally hit another guy in his car but it was really his fault except he showed up in court with a neck brace and it all seemed hopeless until Honorable Father use Honorable Noodle and threw his briefcase on the floor causing Uncle Fester (or at least it was the same actor that played Uncle Fester) to turn quickly proving to the judge that he was a big fat poopy pants liar and Bobby and Cindy were so relieved because they didn't have to testify against their own mother but they DID want to ask the judge to settle the argument they were having in the car when they didn't see their mom turn and look over her shoulder, just as he was doing now.

"Awwww, *crap!*" thought Jack…"holy cow, I put people into this! I have to be waaaay more careful. I got so carried away, like I was in my own little world and forgot about what

I was doing...no people!" He carefully deleted that last paragraph. He would hate to have been responsible for the death of Florence Henderson. Jack rewrote it.

> He put the clunker in reverse, looking over his shoulder in a vain attempt to see through the six-month-overdue-for-washing rear window. At least this way, if he hit something, he could in all honesty claim that he looked over his shoulder and didn't see anything. He was, if nothing else, an honest man.

Somehow, Jack knew instinctively that he had done enough. He had written enough to quell the compulsion. He scanned through the blog entry one more time, to completely make sure there was nothing in there that could be dangerous, that could be linked to an actual person. He held his breath, nervously, as he hit the "submit" key, posting his blog for all the world, and whatever force was seemingly controlling him, to see.

Chapter 13

Jack wasn't woken by the phone. Nor was he woken by sirens outside his window. No, this time, Jack was woken by the sound of screeching brakes and the tremendous crash of metal on metal.

Jack flew out of bed and rushed to the window. There, immediately below his window, was a yellow taxi; more accurately, what was left of a yellow taxi, that had apparently smashed full speed directly into…Jack's parked car. Jack was dumbfounded. He loved that car. He had bought it back during his days at the web startup, just after the IPO. He paid cash; cash he had gotten from his very first sale of stock. That white Cadillac had all the bells and whistles available back in the Internet Heyday, and he had treasured it…Jack stopped his reminiscence short. White Cadillac, totaled from the side. Oh jeez, it couldn't be. Not again.

He was shaken out of it by the sound of yelling down in the street. "Hey, there's a guy in the car! I think he's still alive, get him out of that cab!" Jack rushed to the phone, called 911, and hurriedly gave them his address and a brief synopsis of the situation. He then threw on a robe and rushed downstairs and into the street, to see if he could help. After all, it was the least he could do, since it was entirely his fault.

There was not much to be done downstairs. The guy in the cab was groaning, obviously in pain, but alive. There was no sign of fire or imminent explosion, so the small crowd decided to leave him in the cab until the paramedics arrived; no sense risking spinal injuries. An ambulance and a fire truck arrived within a few minutes, followed closely by a couple of police cars. Jack watched the commotion as the taxi driver was carefully extracted from the cab and strapped to a gurney, then rolled into an ambulance and driven off, lights and sirens blaring.

Jack stood watching as the ambulance disappeared around the corner. He jumped, as he suddenly felt a meaty hand on his shoulder. "Hey, Jack...that your Caddy?" asked Detective Sanderson. Jack was taken aback for a few moments, not sure what to say.

"How did you..." stammered Jack.

"I heard it on the scanner. The address they gave was yours, so I thought I'd head down here, see if you were okay. You okay?"

"Not really...I wrote a blog entry last night, about a car..."

"Yeah, I read it. White Caddy, huh? Look, I know everything so far has been kinda freakily coincidental, but this one is a bit of a stretch, don't ya think? You didn't hardly mention anything, just a scratch on a car. This is something completely different, not even in the same league. Don't beat yourself up over it. C'mon, let's go sit down somewhere where we can chat and have a bite to eat, what do you say? Tell you what, I'll even drive..."

*   *   *   *   *

Sanderson stayed with Jack for the rest of the day. The guy was visibly shaken, and vacillated between stony silence and rambling incoherence. As far as Sanderson could make out, Jack had experienced some unusual, eerie stuff last night with his computer, when it would turn itself on by itself. Sanderson figured it was probably just nerves, or sleeping pills, or both. In any case, Sanderson wanted to make sure Jack was going to be all right. They got a bit of good news shortly after lunch; the cabbie had a few broken bones and was bruised up pretty bad, but he was going to be okay. Jack seemed visibly relieved by this news, as would anyone, but *not* just because the guy was going to be okay. Jack started getting excited about the fact that (in his mind) his blog wasn't always deadly, just destructive. After that, Jack started calming down just a bit, and slowly, as the day dragged on, started getting back to normal.

"Maybe you should just stay at my place tonight," said Sanderson, "that way, I can keep you away from the computer, and you will see that this is all just a very strange series of coincidences."

Jack thought about it. It *did* make some sense – a guy like Sanderson could easily make sure Jack didn't get into any mischief with the computer. "Are you sure the wife won't mind?" he asked.

"Nah, she took the kids down to her mother's for the week, so I'm a bachelor for a few more days anyway. Come on; it'll be fine."

Sanderson drove Jack to his house in the suburbs, to a quiet tree-lined street named Bay Avenue. As they approached the area, Jack couldn't help noticing what a nice neighborhood it was. Not ritzy or expensive, just clean and well maintained. Wide streets, lots of trees, and it seemed like every house had a manicured lawn and a tasteful flower bed. But just before they got to Sanderson's house, there was one glaring exception.

The house had obviously not been painted in decades. The lawn was not a lawn, but a waist-high morass of weeds and junk – an old washing machine, a rusted shopping cart, and ironically a broken push-mower. One of the front windows was broken and had cardboard taped over it, and instead of blinds the window had an old torn sheet tacked up. Various symbols and slogans had been spray painted on the garage door and along the front walk of the house, and Jack suspected these were gang-related. In all, the kind of house you would least expect in a nice neighborhood, but would be par for the course in the worst.

"Whoa! What's up with that?" Jack asked.

Sanderson scowled. "Damn crack house. We've busted the place up a dozen times, but they still come back. Not much we can do from a legal standpoint, either; Lord knows I've tried. Out of town slumlord renting it out as a halfway house. The school the kids go to is only two blocks away, but I have to drive them every morning – no way am I having them walk past this dump, with whatever cracked-out scum may be hanging around it at the moment. Well, here we are!"

Sanderson pulled up to a well-kempt light blue house, with a stereotypical white picket fence and a smooth as glass lawn. It reminded Jack of every other well-kempt house on the block with a stereotypical white picket fence and a smooth as glass lawn. Sanderson ushered Jack inside, and gave him a quick tour.

"Over here's the bathroom, the kitchen's in there. You

can stay in the den here, and my room is here, just up the hall. There's a TV in the den if you want to watch the tube tonight. The computer's in the den, also, but it's dial up, and I'm not giving you the password. So, it's perfectly safe. Over here..."

Jack heard Sanderson talking, but the words weren't making sense. He had them tuned out, nothing was sinking in. He just stood there in the doorway to the den, looking in at the computer on the oak roll-top desk. Jack knew he was in trouble.

"...so what do you think? Jack? Jack??" Sanderson hadn't noticed his guest had stopped listening, he had just kept going. "Jack, are you all right?"

Jack snapped out of it. "Uh, yeah. Yeah, just fine, sure. Sorry, I'm just a bit frazzled and tired, it's been a really long day."

"Yeah, I suppose so. Look, it's starting to get dark, so let me whip up a little dinner – barbecued steaks sound okay? We can pop open a bottle of wine, and afterwards you can hit the hay. Sound good?"

"Yeah. Good." Jack answered. But Jack knew that as nice as the evening sounded, the night was going to be far from good.

Chapter 14

Jack tossed and turned on the rollaway bed in the den that night. He had pretty much polished off a whole bottle of wine by himself at dinner, and not being a very big drinker, he had really felt the effects. He had fallen asleep almost instantly as his head hit the pillow, but it was a restless sleep, and deep inside he knew that it wouldn't last for long. It was only a few hours when he awoke to the pale glow that suffused the room. He knew where the glow came from without even looking, and his heart sank at the prospect.

He sat up, and saw the glowing computer screen on the desk. Of course, he thought, it was already at the blog entry screen. So much for dial up and passwords, grimaced Jack, Sanderson obviously didn't know what he was up against.

Of course, reasoned Jack, *neither do I.*

Jack rolled out of the rollaway, and shuffled, defeated, towards the computer. There was no use fighting it, he knew that. He couldn't resist it, and if he called out to Sanderson, the detective would probably just think he had hacked his way into the computer. And even if Sanderson *had* taken it away, Jack knew that somehow, some way, he would find himself confronted with computer access. It was inevitable. So…why fight it?

But those thoughts gave Jack an idea. What was that old saw, "If you can't beat 'em, join 'em"? Maybe he could turn this situation around. He knew he couldn't resist making an entry, and he knew that the entry would have decimating results to the subject (or one of the subjects) in the blog entry. But, what if Jack were to *use* that for his own purposes? What if he were to try to direct the negative flow where he wanted, instead of just letting it happen randomly? Jack knew what he needed to try.

Blog Entry Number Six:

The cold night wind swept over the decrepit house in the middle of Bay Avenue. This was perhaps the only sweeping that the house had experienced in the last decade. And, truth be told, the house wasn't exactly in the middle of Bay Avenue, since then it would be more of a Road Divider than a House. But it was mid-block. Although it probably would have made a better Divider than a House, with as bad shape as it was in. Not that it had a bad shape; the actual shape was a pretty standard house-type shape; walls, roof, stuff like that. But the shape as in "condition" of the house was dismal. It wasn't the "dark" sort of dismal, although the peeling paint had faded from what was once perhaps a cheery yellow into an unsightly dun color, but more of the depressing, rotting form of the word dismal. In fact it was literally depressing, because the unmaintained structure was sinking in on its own termite-ridden foundation, and those same termites, in addition to other wood-distressing ailments, made the whole place rotting.

The house was so out of place in the otherwise pristine neighborhood, that it was as if this particular house existed in a vacuum. Though, once again, "vacuum" is not something the house was any longer familiar with. Ok, let's get this over with. Words that did *not* apply to this house: sweep, vacuum, clean, paint (unchipped), bright, cheery, well-maintained (okay that's two words, but still...), mowed, upkeep, homey, comfortable, safe, uncrumbly, livable, non-rat-infested, uncondemned, palatial, desirable, quaint, cozy, habitable, neighborly, not-on-the-Police-Department's-most-watched-list. Ok, maybe that last one was a bit of a stretch, word-wise, but the idea holds true.

This was a big gamble, Jack thought...was it worth it? But on the other hand, he had to try *something*. He knew from experience that not writing something was not an option. So, really, he was left with little choice, he reasoned. He had to try, and he had to be very, very careful while doing it.

Nobody ever went into the house. At least, nobody that anybody ever saw. But still, there were telltale signs of human existence. Graffiti scrawled across the walls, garbage strewn about the walkways, empty beer bottles thrown on the lawn, and a few not so empty beer bottles that one could only surmise no longer had beer in them. Newspapers were still delivered to the house, but often piled up in the cracked walkway for weeks at a time. Occasionally, a car would be parked in the driveway, but seemingly never the same car twice. The one thing the various beat up cars that showed up there had in common was their propensity to leak oil all over the stained driveway.

Jack sat back, and read what he had written. Good – nothing about any people, really. Signs of people, perhaps, but nothing specific about anybody that could possibly be pinned down. His mouse hovered over the submit button. He instinctively knew that he had written enough, though he couldn't tell you *how* he knew. But the driving force wasn't pushing him, so he felt safe to end the entry. Was this going to work, he wondered? Was this his escape from the compulsion, or at least from the horrendous consequences of the compulsion? Only one way to find out, really. Jack hit the "submit" button, and sent the blog entry into the ether. What the hell.

Chapter 15

Once again, Jack was awakened by the sounds of screaming sirens. Only this time, he was not surprised by it. In fact he laid in the rollaway bed for a while, and a slight smile, barely perceptible but there nonetheless crept over his lips. Within a few minutes, Sanderson came bounding into the room, pulling on a tattered robe as he came.

"Get up, Jack! Some sort of excitement up the street!"

Jack got up, slipped on his pants and a shirt, shoved his feet into his shoes without bothering about socks, and followed Sanderson through the house and out the front door.

"There!" shouted Sanderson, "Come on!" Jack hurriedly followed his friend a few houses up the block, and stopped just short of the commotion. The commotion was in fact two fire engines and a dozen fire fighters, hurriedly hooking up hoses and deploying equipment and men. A quick glance showed them why: the old crack house was on fire. Totally ablaze would be a more accurate description, thought Jack. The black smoke billowed up into the lazy morning sky, blocking out the early rays just starting to reach into the neighborhood. From inside the conflagration, small explosions could be heard every few minutes, the sound of glass and metal punctuating the roar of the blaze. "Lab equipment." said Sanderson, as yet another crash pierced the sounds of sirens and yelling.

"Anybody in there hurt?" Sanderson asked the Fire Chief, flashing his badge to show he wasn't just another annoying bystander, but an *official* annoying bystander.

"No, we're pretty sure they all got out. Damn, looks like they had a lot of chemicals in there! This could take a while, and we need to clear people back...no telling what fumes we could be dealing with!"

Jack and Sanderson backed away, joining the ever growing crowd whose eyes were unwaveringly glued to the scene. They watched for about forty five minutes, until there was not much left of the old place but some simmering embers and charred wreckage. Sanderson was visibly agitated, wavering between relief that the blight on the neighborhood was gone, and concern over what had happened. After all, a huge fire just a few doors down was certainly a scary prospect.

Jack, however, was strangely calm. In fact, he had to admit to himself, he hadn't felt this at ease in several days. He smiled a sort of Mona Lisa, half hidden smile to himself, knowing that he, Jack, had taken it upon himself to rid the neighborhood of the travesty of the crack house. He knew, *knew*, he could control the power now. He had proven it, hadn't he? Wasn't this exactly what he had hoped for, what he had planned on achieving? He could shape the results, a bit, at least, but enough to control the consequences of his blog, and actually do some good. He had never really considered himself a philanthropist or a Good Samaritan or anything, but now...Jack enjoyed the feeling of helping, even if it was through a destructive force, and even if it was through a mostly uncontrollable medium.

Yessiree, Jack thought, *I'm not such a bad guy after all*, as he watched the firemen start to pack up their things and clean up the scene.

"You *what?*" Sanderson nearly yelled later that morning. "What do you *mean* you talked about that house on your blog last night? That's impossible!"

"I woke up, and the computer was on, logged in. I didn't *want* to turn it on, and I didn't, it was just…on."

"Look, Jack, not only did I not give you the password, but I took the precaution of removing the plug wire and putting it in another room. Just look!"

Sanderson lead Jack into the den and to the computer desk. Sure enough, looking behind the computer, there was no power cord. It was a desktop computer, so there was no battery from which it could have run, either. Apparently, what Jack had done *was* impossible, though by now, not even this surprised Jack.

*   *   *   *   *

The detective went out of the room for a moment, then came back with the power cord. He plugged it into the back of the computer, then slipped the prongs into the wall plug receptacle. A quick push of the Power button, and within a few minutes the computer was up and running. Sanderson navigated to Jack's blog page (he had it bookmarked under his "Fun Stuff" folder), and brought up last night's entry.

"Well I'll be…" Sanderson stammered. The date and time stamp were from about 2am last night. Just like Jack had said. And the entry certainly was about that house, no doubt about it. Sanderson started wondering to himself if maybe Jack wasn't having some schizophrenic episodes or something, and had set the fire himself. But what about the power cord? Then Sanderson reasoned it was possible that Jack had happened to have one with him, after all, they are all the same standard cord. But what were the odds of that? Oh hell, what were the odds of *anything* in this whole crazy episode?

Then it dawned on Sanderson that this couldn't be the case. As a detective, especially a rather well-known detective with a family, Sanderson insisted on having one of the most up to date home security systems available. This meant that not only could no intruder get in without Sanderson, the neighbors, and half the city's police force knowing...but nobody could go *out* either, once the system was armed. And Sanderson knew damn well that the system had been armed last night and this morning – Jack could *not*, in any way that Sanderson could fathom, have gotten out to set that fire.

So, was this just another in a long string of nearly inconceivable coincidences, wondered Sanderson? Or maybe Jack was on to something...maybe it was as weird as his friend had claimed...No, impossible. But...Sanderson was getting a headache just thinking about it. He had never gone in for psychics or tarot or horoscopes or any of that crap, so why was he even *considering* this possibility now? Why? Because he was a detective, and he couldn't come up with any alternate scenarios. After all, as Sherlock Holmes, though fictional, had once said, "When you have eliminated all which is impossible, then whatever remains, however improbable, must be the truth."

The question was, really, which explanation for all this was the impossible one?

Chapter 16

"Okay, Jack, are you *sure* you haven't told anyone about this?" asked the detective. "No? Good; they would just think you were crazy anyway. Heck, they would think I was crazy for not thinking you were crazy!"

"Don't worry. I haven't said a word. I didn't even mean to tell *you*, except you beat it out of me in your interrogation room!" Jack smiled. Sanderson had never been anything but pleasant and cordial to Jack, even before they got to know each other, but it was Jack's nature to inflict a little good natured jest once in a while. "So, what do we do now?"

"Well, if what you say is true, Jack, then you have to write. Things are going to conspire to give you the opportunity, under most circumstances, and once the opportunity is available, your irresistible compulsion will kick in. So, we have two choices, really. Beat it, or use it. And I don't really know what the best choice is."

"Maybe since we don't know for sure what to do, the most prudent course is to do nothing." continued Sanderson. "No, I know you think this isn't possible, and maybe it isn't, but we can give it a try...but it might be a bit unpleasant for you, Jack."

"What are you talking about? What do you have in mind?"

"Well, the problem, it seems to me, is that you are being given the opportunity to post, so you post. Not your fault, I understand that – sounds to me like you have done everything in your power to fight it. But that's kind of the point…you have only done the things in *your* power to avoid it…maybe it's time to apply some of *my* power as well."

"Uh, Sanderson, I'm not sure I'm liking the sound of this…"

"Jack, you ever hear of a 'Panic Room'?"

"Wasn't that the movie with Jodie Foster? Yeah, I liked that one…"

"Well, if you saw the movie, then you know what I am talking about. It turns out I have a Panic Room. When you're a detective, and you want to take care of your family, you can't be too careful – lots of crazies I've locked up would love to get a little revenge, you know what I mean? Anyway, down in the basement, I have a secure room, plenty comfortable, but nobody goes in, and nobody goes out without me letting them. Understand?"

"Yeah," sighed Jack, "you want to lock me up, keep me out of mischief. I don't know, sounds kind of…twisted, really. I'm just not sure about this, Sanderson."

"Well what are our other options, Jack? Give you free reign to blog your little heart out, and sit back and let the consequences fall where they may?"

"You've got a point there, I guess. But what about going forward? This might be okay for a night or two, but you can't lock me up in that cell… sorry, Panic Room forever…can you?"

"No, and I really don't know how this is going to play out in the long run. But let's just give it a shot, to see if we *can* beat this, even for just a little bit. For all we know, all we need to do is break the cycle to get rid of the...rid of this..."

"Curse," finished Jack. "This is a curse, go ahead and say it."

"Okay, curse. Damn, I can't believe I'm actually falling into this whole morass. But anyway, maybe this will change something. Worth a shot, right? I mean, not really any downside to it, is there?"

"Nope," agreed Jack, "you're right...what the hell!"

That evening, after all the necessary preparations had been made, the reinforced steel door clicked shut, with Jack on the inside and Sanderson on the outside. Jack sucked in his breath, a sudden wave of claustrophobia sweeping over him which subsided as he got mental control over himself.

"Just breathe, Jack, that's all you have to do...breathe steadily, deeply..." Jack told himself. Once his nerves calmed a bit, Jack looked around. There was not much in the Panic Room; it was made for practicality, not for comfort. There was a sink, a microwave, and a small refrigerator in one corner. In another corner was a very small enclosed area that Jack could only presume was the bathroom.

The off-white ceiling matched the rest of the off-white room, and was bare except for a single light fixture and a smoke detector. A cot, a couch, and a coffee table rounded out the accoutrements of the tiny cubicle. Other cots were stacked up in one more corner; those must be for the rest of Sanderson's family, Jack thought. A few TV monitors were mounted up on the wall, with a small remote control lying on the coffee table. Sanderson had explained to Jack that the TVs, in addition to being hooked up to the cable network, were also hooked up to security cameras peppered around the house and grounds. If Sanderson was holed up in here, he wanted to know where the bad guys were on the outside.

The only other thing that really stood out in the room was the door. Big, gray, and metal, it was not at all a cheery thing. An enclosure for some bolting mechanism ran the width of the door halfway down; you could tell it was no ordinary deadbolt. It was massive, and the size of the enclosure told Jack that some pretty sophisticated electronics were inside it controlling the darn thing. All in all, it was a door that told you in a single glance: I'm closed. Nobody, good guy or bad, was getting through that thing while it was locked.

Jack slumped down on the couch, grabbed the remote, and flipped on a TV. He browsed around the channels for a while, but couldn't concentrate. Not a good sign, he told himself. Then he decided to try the other TVs. He switched those on, and started figuring out the remote control, to see how to switch views from camera to camera throughout the house and grounds. There on the leftmost monitor was the front door and entry hall. The right hand monitor showed the back door and porch. Flipping around, Jack was able to see the master bedroom, the kids' rooms, playroom, living room, and the infernal den where he had spent the previous night. One more channel showed a panoramic view of the front yard, and yet another showed a similar view of the back. Jack had to smile, despite the tension, when the kitchen camera showed Sanderson's backside sticking out of the fridge as he foraged for a snack. Amazing that such a big man could get so far into a fridge, Jack mused. Sanderson must have sensed he was being watched, or perhaps the blinking red light on the camera gave Jack away, but in any case, Sanderson extracted himself from the fridge, turned around, and with an impish grin on his face, flipped his meaty middle finger off at the camera. Jack laughed for the first time in hours.

A few hours of mindless TV later, Jack decided it was time to hit the cot. Nothing strange had happened, nothing untoward. No urges or uncontrollable cravings for blogging. Jack was a little surprised by this; he had fully expected to be somewhat of a raving lunatic by this time, pounding on the door and pleading for online access at any cost. Hmm, he thought, maybe the craving is based on availability…maybe it wasn't triggered because it realized inevitable defeat. Maybe Jack was being an idiot anthropomorphizing a craving. He lay down on the cot, pulled a blanket over himself, and slowly drifted off into an uneasy slumber.

Jack was awoken by a vaguely familiar buzzing sound that permeated the otherwise still and slightly stale air of the Panic Room. He sat up in the dark room, not knowing where he was for a few moments, completely disoriented. His situation eventually came back to him, and he fumbled around trying to determine where the buzzing was coming from. Then it struck him. The buzzing was from his cell phone…he had his cell phone with him, and he had forgotten all about it! He had his…web-enabled smart phone.

The buzzing stopped. Jack knew that it wasn't somebody trying to call him. He knew that it was just a way to remind him of the cell phone... something, whatever or whoever was doing this to him, wanted him to know he wasn't off the hook.

Of course, Jack tried to fight it. Despite the fact he knew it was hopeless. He threw the cell phone against the steel door, but amazingly, the phone was undamaged. He put it in the refrigerator, trying to ignore it, but he could still hear the buzzing. The buzzing wasn't from the phone, though, he knew it was in his head…it was going to keep going, unstoppable, until he did the inevitable. He took it out of the freezer, tried to shut it off. It went off, only to flash back on moments later. He turned it off again. A flicker, and it was back on. He tried to take the battery off the back of the damn phone, but it wouldn't budge. It was truly hopeless. Jack knew there was a web device at his disposal (despite the fact that he couldn't dispose of it), and he felt the panic and frenzy welling up inside himself.

So he tried to open the door. The big gray metal door. He banged on it, naturally to no avail. He threw all his weight into it, smashing his shoulder, but in vain. Pound, pound, pound as he might, not a budge. There was not an iota of movement from the door, despite Jack's hardest and most painful efforts. He was panicking; he knew it, but he also knew he could not stop the panic. The door prevented his escape. The cell phone called him, both figuratively and literally, and he knew he could not escape the call, not while the door barred his way. He looked at his hands…a few rivulets of blood washed across his palms, over his wrists, and were soaking into the cuffs of his shirt – he had pounded his fists against the metal door to the point of bleeding. He felt no pain, surprisingly, but the sight of his blood made him shiver and the panic welled even higher.

Finally, the dam burst. Jack couldn't stop it – it just flooded over him, washing him away despite his best efforts. He was insane at that moment; he knew it. He turned the small screen on, pressed the buttons to log onto the web, and used the inconvenient keypad to navigate to his blog entry page.

Blog Entry Number Seven

the damn door the big steel door the door dor dooor stood in the way of escape there was no escape there was no way ou7 of the r00m trapp3d in the room becausf of the do0r and it would no7 open no sir33 it was locked and a huge lock electronic thing barring the way no way all the way cvant get out of the room I wish the door wasn't there because I want out o u t out get me out of here past the door past the lock past the mechanism that bars my escape bars barring my way way out it is way out of her to the way out of here I can7 wait to be gone goone get along little doggie for the door it calls to you and you must heed the call but the door isnt doing the calling it is the other side of the door the door is what is keeping the calling from being a sucesful call it is failing me n this my worst hour because my hour is nearly up and I want out of the room and out of the door and ut of the lock and out of the bar and into a bar oh yes a dirnk in a bar but not a metal bar because the metal bar is holding the door not holding a drink and I want a drink but not a door 200 who is doing this to me why me the door the door is keeping me from escaping the dor is stopping my fligh7 out of here and I don't w4nt to be here I don't want to type I need help me help me help me help me the door s gray and metal and large and heavy and so very heavy and strong and I am not strong becasuem I cannot escape a simple door I am smarter than the door arent I tehn why cant I get past it like I should be able to figure out a way but the door is locking and mocking me and an electronic moc lock is stopping me i hurt let me go let my mind go let me go past the door that is all I ask I do not want anything else I swear I just want to go the door stops me damn door damn the door die door die go away do not sotp me any more door do not door me any stop doorstop doorstop hey that's funny i made a joke doorstop because the door stops me but I cannot stop worrying about the door door door door door door door door door door door door door door door door door door d00r d00r d00rd 00r d00r door dooor dor door dor door door oor door door door doord oor door door doooooor

Jack did not know what he was typing, the flood of panic had swept over him so fully. The keypad of the cell phone was slick with the blood of his cut and broken hands, and still he typed, numbly, yet quickly. Quicker than he knew possible on such a device. His frenzy went unabated until suddenly, it stopped. Jack paused, stared weakly at the phone's small screen, and hit the "submit" key. He shut the screen on the phone, then fell unconscious to the floor.

He was startled by the sound of the fire alarm. From the time on his phone, he knew he had been out for only a few minutes, but apparently, a lot had happened in those few minutes. He quickly looked around to ascertain the situation, and in the back of his mind he knew he was back to his old, sane self again. At least for the moment.

The fire alarm was shrilling its warning at a deafening level. It had been set off by a column of smoke that billowed out of the mechanism holding the door shut. The door. The damn door. He vaguely remembered that he had ranted about the door on the blog. Now, through the smoke surrounding the door, he could see flashes of blue sparks, and licks of flames coming from the housing around the door's mechanism. And somehow, above the din of the smoke alarm, he could hear another sound. Pounding. Someone was pounding on the other side of the metal door. It was faint, to be sure, due to the thickness of the door, but Jack heard it nonetheless. Sanderson, it had to be Sanderson! He had heard the sound of the alarm, and had come trying to get Jack out of there.

Jack quickly ran to the door, and despite the heat and smoke, gave a tremendous kick with the bottom of his foot at the latch of the door. He heard a snap, and for a moment thought it was his foot breaking. But it was the door...the heat and sparks and whatever malfunction was causing all this had left the door almost opened, and Jack's kick had finished the job. The bolt was open now, and suddenly the door swung open revealing a haggard and panicked Sanderson staring in from the other side. Jack rushed out the door, past the gasping Sanderson, and fell in a heap on the floor. Sanderson quickly remembered the fire extinguisher that he was holding limply by his side, and with a few well-placed bursts of the white cloud, put out the flames in the door housing and quelled the smoke. Danger averted.

After a few moments, Jack hauled himself up off the floor, the panic gone from his face, only to be replaced by a look of consternation. Sanderson was relieved that his friend was okay, but he just didn't know what to make of the situation.

"What the hell happened in there?" he asked. But he knew the answer. He had been awake, on the computer, trying to make sense of Jack's situation, when his RSS feed had informed him of a new entry on Jack's blog. He had thought it impossible...he had removed the old clunker desktop computer from the Panic Room while preparing for Jack's stay in there, and there was just no other way to get online access in there. "I saw your blog entry, but how...?"

"Web phone. Wave of the future." Said Jack dryly, holding up the device. Then, with a sudden burst of anger, he threw his cell phone against the wall. This time, it smashed into a dozen pieces. Why couldn't it have done that before?

Chapter 17

"So *now* what?" asked Jack, as he and Sanderson sat in the small café, drinking coffee and unenthusiastically nibbling on bagels. "I can't fight this, Sanderson. I've tried, I've tried everything. But no matter *what* I try...*it happens*." Jack never looked up, instead staring into the inky blackness of his coffee. "Now what..." he trailed off.

Sanderson took a deep breath. He had been thinking about it all morning, naturally. He knew what he had to do, but he was having a hard time coming to terms with it. It was against Sanderson's nature to give up, to bail on a friend. But what he was dealing with here, well, *it* certainly wasn't natural. It wasn't something he could help with, anyway, he told himself. He was just a detective, a plain old cop-on-the-street...how could he be expected to know what to do in a bizarre situation like this? But he's a friend, a voice in his head kept saying...he needs you, he needs somebody, just somebody to believe him, to not give up. Sanderson quickly squelched that voice, though, with a simple thought: his family.

Jack was dangerous, perhaps the most dangerous person

Sanderson had ever known despite a life spent around criminals. He didn't worry about himself; no cop with the years he had in the line of fire could; but his *family*. He knew that all it would take is one little mention in that blog, and his wife and kids could be put in harm's way – could be literally sentenced to death. Sentenced to death…that phrase just took on a whole new meaning, Sanderson wryly mused.

"Jack…I have to tell you something. I can't help you, I don't know what to do or who to turn to any more than you do, but…well, we have to stop seeing each other."

Jack laughed, for the first time that day. "You make it sound like we're breaking up! I never knew you *felt* that way, Sanderson!" Jack teased his friend.

"Jack, it isn't funny. I have my family to think of, and, well, you're a keg of dynamite just waiting to explode. I can't hang around you, I can't help you, I just can't be your friend anymore…"

Jack nodded grimly. "Really, Sanderson, I understand. I can't and don't blame you. The *good* news is, now I *know* you believe me, you believe what is happening to me. At least that's something."

Sanderson suddenly stood up, turned away, and started walking. A few steps, and he turned around: "Goodbye, Jack. Good luck. I mean that." And the detective walked out of Jack's life.

*   *   *   *   *

Jack once again stared into his now cold coffee. He knew their parting had been inevitable. He was alone, nobody knew what he was going through, and there was no way he would be able to convince anybody of his bizarre…what *was* it? A "situation"? An "affliction"? Anyway, it wouldn't matter even if he could convince somebody, because there was nothing anybody could do about it. And he asked himself one more time, "*Now* what?" Only this time, there was nobody there to hear.

Chapter 18

Blog Entry Number Eight

The silent, cold killer silently and coldly slunk through the silent, cold alley. He was cold, but he remained silent. The temperature was dropping as night fell, and the ambient noise in the Baypoint District, where he slunk, was several decibels below the norm. He hadn't struck for a week or more, and the need to kill was mounting in his brain. "They'll never catch me…they'll never catch me…I'm smarter than them." This was his mantra, and the fact that he had struck and killed six times before made him believe it.

Jack was sweating. This had to work; this had to be why he was here and why he had been "afflicted". He couldn't stop the blogging; that he now knew. His only choice was to try to control it. If he was going to be destructive, he needed to try to be destructive towards those things that needed destruction. The Baypoint Killer had been terrorizing that district for months, and, as far as Jack knew, the police were stumped. Well, if good old fashioned police work wasn't going to do it, maybe Jack's penchant for destruction with his blog would. Maybe this was also a way to thank Sanderson for believing him. All he had to do was make sure he stayed *focused* on the object, the killer, and not let his words stray.

He knew they would never find him here. This alley was nowhere near any of the other places he had struck, so why would the police be looking here? He also knew it was a shortcut between the Financial District and a bunch of good, cheap local restaurants. There was always some rich banker-type who stayed late at work and wanted a quick meal. He was counting on that. He settled in between a couple of overflowing dumpsters, hidden in the deepening shadows and occasionally blowing on his hands to keep them warm and ready. He didn't have long to wait.

He heard the heavy clumping of footsteps coming up the alley before he actually saw anyone. Just one man, large but unaware of danger. The perfect victim. He would do the same thing he had done with all the other victims – just before walking past, he would spring up and plunge the long, thin, and extremely sharp dagger right through the sternum. Sure, it would be safer to strike from behind, but it was just so satisfying to see the surprised look on the victim's face, followed by the fear, the pain, and finally the blankness. So many emotions in just a few seconds, who could resist? He was still, not daring to even breathe lest he give away his presence. Closer, closer, just a few more feet, one more step, and...

There was no sound as the killer leapt up, arm cocked and ready. It was so much more fun to be silent, so much more intriguing. The victim flinched at the sight of the springing assailant, but there was not time to do anything before the dagger struck – no turning away, no hands rising in defense, no screaming. The force of the blow was tremendous; the killer was well practiced, and knew his business. But what the killer wasn't expecting was the blade snapping as it struck something hard. The reverberation of the break shot up his arm like an electric charge, both hurting and numbing his hand and arm up to the shoulder.

"Wha…" was all the killer could get out before he heard a voice behind him yell, "Freeze!" The erstwhile victim had been knocked to the ground with the violence of the attack, but his body armor had protected him, and he was starting to rouse himself to his feet. The voice behind him must have been yet another cop, for obviously, that was what the victim was – a stinking undercover cop!

Without a word, the killer leaped past the half-risen victim, hoping speed and surprise would win his escape. Two shots rang out in the no longer silent but still cold alley, and they found their mark. The killer whirled with the impact, fell, skidded a few feet, tensed, shivered, then relaxed, as the world went dark, and cold, and silent…

Jack read back to himself what he had just written. "Damn," he said to himself, "I got carried away again! There's too much in there about the cops. I better rewrite that." He moved the mouse over the "delete entry" icon on the screen, and clicked.

He gaped at the screen. To his horror, instead of the "Deleting Entry…" message he was expecting to see, the screen flashed "Uploading Entry…10%…

40%…70%…100%…Entry Posted Successfully."

He stared at the screen for minutes. His mind was a blank, he couldn't focus; he could barely even breathe. What had he done? Eventually, he gained control of himself. He had to get hold of Sanderson. He wasn't sure why, but he just knew he *had* to get hold of him, tell him about the blog entry.

He called Sanderson's direct line at the station. Five rings, six, seven, then a female voice picked up the line. "Detective Sanderson's office. Jessica speaking. Can I help you?" Jessica must be the secretary for the department, thought Jack. "Uh, yeah…" Jack stammered. "I'm looking for Detective Sanderson. It's pretty urgent. Can I speak to him?"

A moment of silence, then "I'm sorry, the Detective is out on assignment right now. Can I take a message?"

"Please, this is urgent. I need him to call me as soon as humanly possible…my name is Jack Spurling, he has my number."

"Oh, Jack!" said Jessica. "He told me you might be calling. He said to tell you he was out doing a little undercover work this evening, and if all goes well, you might get to see his name in the papers tomorrow…they have a lead on the Baypoint Killer. Hello…hello? Jack? Are you there?"

Chapter 19

Naturally, Jack couldn't sleep that night. What had he done? What had possessed him to think he could control this? Hell, what had possessed him, period? He paced through the night, occasionally checking the TV news channels to see if there was any word of happenings in the Baypoint District. He knew he should be checking the news sites on the Internet, but he didn't have the nerve to go anywhere near his computer.

Finally, a story broke on Channel 7's "News in the Morning".

The reporter who co-anchored the show looked straight into the camera and read from her teleprompter.

"We have just learned that the notorious Baypoint Killer, blamed for the deaths of six people in the Baypoint District, has been killed. Police set up a daring undercover operation last night, luring the killer into a trap. We are awaiting official word from the Police Commissioner, but our sources tell us that the killer was gunned down by police as he tried to escape. Our sources also tell us that one officer was wounded in the battle, but...wait...this just in...we now have official word from Police Headquarters confirming the story.

"The Baypoint killer has been killed. Detective Larry Sanderson, the detective credited with tracking the killer and setting up the operation, was stabbed during the encounter, and is now in critical condition at Mercy Hospital. Doctors say his condition is grave, and don't hold much hope...."

Jack didn't hear any more of the story as he slumped into the sofa. He had killed his friend. The only person to believe him, and Jack had killed him. He thought he could *control* what would happen. *Control* it, for crying out loud...what was he thinking?

And it dawned on him. He couldn't win. He couldn't resist it, and he couldn't control it. He was absolutely helpless, and doomed to wreak havoc and death. There was no escape. None. He would always be compelled to type on whatever device was available, and he would always be compelled to seek out a device.

He thought about moving far away, in the country somewhere, with no electricity, but quickly discarded that idea. He knew, with absolute certainty, that he would be compelled to come back, to *find* a place with a computer. Any place he could get to, he would find a way back, and find a way to type. And anything, anything at all that he typed about would face destruction.

There was no avoiding it, just as long as it was possible to...and suddenly, to his horror, Jack knew what he had to do. He knew how to end the curse, how to prevent any more death. But was he brave enough to do it? Could he actually go through with it? He thought about Sanderson, lying, most likely dying, in Mercy Hospital, and he knew he had to.

Jack walked to his computer, slowly, like a condemned man walking towards a gallows. He sat in the chair, flicked on the monitor. Naturally, the screen was already somehow on the blog entry screen – he had of course been expecting that. He cracked his knuckles, took a deep breath, and forced himself to concentrate. He could not afford a mistake, and he could not afford to chicken out. He knew he *had* to stick to one subject, and one subject alone, and *not* leave any room for doubt. There could be no mistaking what was to be doomed, or else the plan would fail, and more innocent deaths would be on his hands.

Blog Entry Number Nine

My hands. My hands. My hands. My hands myhands my hands my hands my hands my hands my hands my hands my hands my hands my hands my hands my hands my hands my hands my hands my hands my handsmy hands my hands my hands my hands my hands my hands my hands my hands my hands my hands my hands my hands my hands my hands my hands my hands my hands My hands my hands my hands my hands my hands my hands my hands my hands my hands my hands my hands my hands myhands my handsMy hands my hands my hands my hands my hands my hands my hands my hands my hands my hands my hands

my hands my hands my hands myhands my hands
my hands my hands my hands my hands my hands
my hands my handsmy hands my hands my hands
my hands my hands my hands my hands my hands
my hands my hands my hands my hands my hands
my hands my hands my hands my hands my hands
my hands my hands my hands my hands myhands
my hands my hands my hands my hands my hands
my hands my hands my hands my hands my hands
my hands my hands my hand my hands my hands
my hands my hands my hands my hands my hands
my hands my hands my hands my hands my hands
my hands my hands my hands my hands my hands
my hands my hands my hands my hands my hands
my hands my hands my hands my hands my hands
my hands my hands my hands my hands my hands
my hands my hands.

Jack took his hands off the keyboard for the last time. He watched his right hand, as he reached for the mouse, and moved it slowly to the "Submit" icon. A deep breath, a silent prayer. "What the hell," he mumbled to himself. Click.

Epilogue

Nancy Francis, Physical Therapist and Personal Assistant, had a surprise for her patient. It had been three months since the terrible accident, the first two of which the patient, Jack, had spent in the hospital, and the last month here at his apartment, where she took care of him. He obviously could not care for himself, given his condition. He was a quiet and morose man, Nancy thought, but no wonder. After what he had been through! She shuddered involuntarily at the thought.

It had been such a bizarre accident. She remembered reading about it in the papers, incredulous at the story, yet here she was, months later, working for the man. I mean, to have both your hands severed by papayas? Well, technically, it was the papaya *display* at the B&G across the street that had suddenly come crashing down, toppling the metal sign above it and sending it plummeting like a guillotine, just as he was reaching for the fruit. What were the odds?

The doctors were unable to do anything. And, strangely, Jack had refused – absolutely refused – any sort of prosthetic devices. He insisted on having only the stumps. That was pretty weird, Nancy thought. He was a computer guru, so everybody had said, and yet he wouldn't get any of the highly advanced modern prosthetics that would allow him to live a somewhat normal life, and even possibly return to work.

But she had a surprise. "Jack, I want you to close your eyes. Yes, close them tight. Good. Now, here, let me lead you…that's right, just to over here. Now, here, have a seat. No, keep them closed. Ok, hold on a second, here we go. I'm just going to put this on over your head…ok, got it. You can open your eyes now! Surprise!"

He opened his eyes, blinked, and took a second to focus. Then, Nancy could have sworn she had seen a momentary look of fear in his eyes. Better explain.

"That's headphones and a microphone on your head, Jack. I just picked this stuff up at the computer store for you, and installed it on your computer. Voice recognition software, Jack!"

And this time there was no mistaking it, thought Nancy. A distinct look of fear.

About the Author:

Mark Berkeland is (against all odds) gainfully employed as a software engineer in San Jose, California, despite a penchant for puns, practical jokes, wordplay, and the occasional Groaner. He attributes this to the fact that most of his technical presentations are completely accurate yet usually in verse, or, verse yet, in song. As a father of 6, he has worked long and hard to perfect the ubiquitous "Dad Joke"; never, *ever* tell him you're getting a haircut, that you're tired, or ask him to make you a sandwich. When not inflicting his misbegotten humor on his long-suffering wife and children, Mr. Berkeland is a Mentor for the local High School's Robotics Team, and is an avid Letterboxer. Blog Post Mortem his first book, though he does have a verified history of annoying his coworkers with extremely long, often fictitious emails.

Connect with me online:

Email: m-berkeland@electric-scroll.com
Facebook: Mark Berkeland
Twitter: @wassamatta_u

Made in the USA
San Bernardino, CA
15 January 2019